REBEL RANGER

Also by William Colt MacDonald in Large Print:

Action at Arcanum
Alias Dix Ryder
Blind Cartridges
The Comanche Scalp
Powdersmoke Range
Ridin' Through
Two-Gun Deputy
King of Crazy River
The Phantom Pass

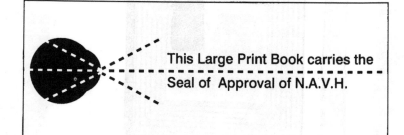

REBEL RANGER

William Colt MacDonald

WHEELER PUBLISHING

Published in 2004 by arrangement with
Golden West Literary Agency.

Wheeler Large Print Western.

The text of this Large Print edition is unabridged.
Other aspects of the book may vary from the original edition.

Set in 16 pt. Plantin by Minnie B. Raven.

Printed in the United States on permanent paper.

Library of Congress Cataloging-in-Publication Data

MacDonald, William Colt, 1891–1968.
    Rebel ranger / William Colt MacDonald.
        p. cm.
     ISBN 1-58724-717-8 (lg. print : sc : alk. paper)
     1. Texas Rangers — Fiction.   2. Texas — Fiction.
   3. Large type books.   I. Title.
    PS3525.A2122R43 2004
    813'.52—dc22   2004042004

REBEL RANGER

As the Founder/CEO of NAVH, the only national health agency solely devoted to those who, although not totally blind, have an eye disease which could lead to serious visual impairment, I am pleased to recognize Thorndike Press★ as one of the leading publishers in the large print field.

Founded in 1954 in San Francisco to prepare large print textbooks for partially seeing children, NAVH became the pioneer and standard setting agency in the preparation of large type.

Today, those publishers who meet our standards carry the prestigious "Seal of Approval" indicating high quality large print. We are delighted that Thorndike Press is one of the publishers whose titles meet these standards. We are also pleased to recognize the significant contribution Thorndike Press is making in this important and growing field.

Lorraine H. Marchi, L.H.D.
Founder/CEO
NAVH

★ Thorndike Press encompasses the following imprints: Thorndike, Wheeler, Walker and Large Print Press.

I. Fence War

One moment the valley had stretched peacefully beneath the occasionally cloud-obscured moon, the nocturnal quiet broken only by the continual shrill yap-yapping of coyotes along the bordering hilltops. Then, as though by some prearranged signal, the sudden cessation of the sharp barking had coincided with the passing of the waning moon below the valley horizon. Darkness settled, and as the final echoes died away to a whisper, the gray-furred beasts slunk silently through the cedar brakes, or halted in frozen-footed fear, sharp eyes and ears intent, sensing, rather than seeing or smelling, the darkly moving man-forms, some mounted, some on foot, at various points on the valley floor below.

A deeper, more menacing darkness closed in on, engulfed, the timbered hills and grassy valley. Time drifted slowly, as though impeded by that hush in which violence and hatred were inexorably mounting to the point of eruption. The coyotes waited, stilled, for what would happen next, as it had happened on other nights. Unmistakably it came, the sudden fierce twang of tightly strung wire

7

abruptly, angrily, released from tension, the high, vibrant tone carrying clearly in the night air across the five-mile reach from valley wall to valley wall.

Thrice more that same incisive sound whined through the stillness as the fence cutters worked with swift efficiency, the twang of the last severed length of barbed wire blending with a hoarse warning cry and a high-pitched challenge, with between the two the savage double roar of a buckshot-loaded shotgun. Instantly, as though again by pre-arranged signal, similar sounds burst from two other points in the valley.

Rifles were exploding now, and six-shooters, tearing wide the gloom with brilliant lances of orange flame. A man cursed, the words choking abruptly in his throat. A horse screamed and went down, kicking, slamming its rider to the hoof-churned earth. The firing continued, then lessened.

After a time it stopped altogether. . . .

Early light grayed the main street of Painted Post. With the single exception of Sheriff Zach Robertson, restlessly pacing the small porch in front of his office, there wasn't a soul to be seen. The hitch racks along the thoroughfare were deserted; doors were still tightly closed. A thin line of crimson was commencing to push up above the eastern horizon.

The sheriff was a bulkily built man with

worried eyes and thin gray hair. One leg of his trousers was tucked into a boot top; the other hung down about his ankle. His woolen shirt was open at the throat; from one pocket of his open vest dangled a Bull Durham tag. He looked as though he hadn't had enough sleep. His harried glance kept searching a well-worn roadway that stretched toward the north and into a long grassy valley.

As he paused momentarily, midway of the porch, the door at his rear opened and a gangling, sleepy-eyed individual with bony features and tousled black hair stepped outside, leaving the doorway to the combination office and sleeping quarters ajar at his back. He surveyed the sheriff, heavy-eyed, a moment, then, in half-humorous complaint, "It don't help my rest none to listen to your clump-clump-clump out here. You training for a foot race?"

Without turning Sheriff Robertson said heavily, "Didn't you hear 'em? The shots, I mean."

"You telling that the Cross-J is cutting fences again?"

"I don't mean nothing else, Obie."

Obie Grant shook his head. "No, I didn't hear any shots, and I don't figure you did either. This business has got you so worked up, your imagination plumb runs away with you. If you'd sleep nights —"

9

"It was quiet, plumb quiet, last night," the sheriff said in a monotone. "Just the coyotes a-heckling at each other. Then they all stopped to once — just like on those other nights when those gunfights took place —"

"Cripes!" Obie jeered. "Just 'cause the coyotes hushed for a spell is no sign there was another fence-cutting ruckus. I ain't sure gunshots would carry this far; the sound, I mean. You sure you heard 'em?"

"What I heard, or what I didn't hear," Robertson said irritably, "makes no difference. It's what I feel, what I know in my bones. I'm telling you there was trouble last night." Obie laughed softly and started to roll a cigarette. He didn't say anything. The sheriff went on, "Trouble with you, you take your responsibilities too light. Hell's due to break loose around here!" For the first time he faced his deputy.

"What do you want me to do, rope it down again?"

Robertson's eyes blazed. "Right there's an example of what I mean: I try to be serious and all you can do is spit out a smart-alecky reply. I don't like it! As a deputy —"

"Just a minute, Zach." Some of the sleepiness faded from Obie Grant's eyes. "Maybe I'm no better satisfied with this deputy job than you are with me. I can't see's there's any use being a law officer when you won't let me act. You can have my badge right now, if you like. All's you'd had to do was give me the go-ahead and I'll move plenty pronto. I'll go to the Cross-J and either enforce the law or —"

"All right, Obie, I'm sorry," Robertson said wearily. He mopped his brow with a faded bandanna. "I reckon when you get down to cases you got a legal kick coming. I'm admitting that I'm at fault, but try to see it my way. Alex Jenkins is a friend of mine. I just can't bring myself to enforce the law where he's concerned. And there's Pat and Brazos — Cripes a'mighty, the whole outfit is like blood relations." He stopped suddenly, then in a hopeless tone, "I reckon if anybody resigns, it better be me. It's just — just that I keep hoping that everything will work out for the good. Each time there's a ruckus I've thought maybe it would be the last. Hell! I'm one poor excuse for a sheriff if there ever was one."

"Quit worrying about it," Obie said. "Maybe things will work out for the best." He didn't sound very hopeful. "If not, Zach, you're just going to have to take firm steps, friendships or no. I'm not telling you your duty; you know that as well as me — and whatever you do, I'm behind you. Hell's bells! I know how you feel." He switched the conversation suddenly. "You sure you heard shots last night?"

Robertson shook his head. "Not sure, no. I

11

just felt 'em, if you know what I mean. And thanks for saying what you did. Don't pay me no attention when I get grumpy. My nerves are sort of frayed out, I reckon."

Grant didn't reply at once. Finally he said in a grim sort of voice, "Maybe you did hear shots last night. Leastwise, I reckon you were right about 'em."

The sheriff's red-rimmed eyes followed the direction of Obie's finger where it pointed along the roadway to the north. A cloud of dust moved swiftly in the direction of Painted Post. There appeared to be a wagon and three or four riders on the way to town.

The sheriff's lined face darkened. "Do you suppose — ?" He left the question unfinished.

Obie said dryly, "Folks don't drive a wagon in this early to buy beans and flour. Nor," he added, "if they did, they wouldn't need any bodyguard."

The sun was just tipping above the hills to the east when the wagon rumbled into town. Two grim-faced cowboys rode on each side of the wagon. On the driver's seat were two more men. All were heavily armed. In the bed of the wagon was a dead man, and stretched on blankets beside him another puncher with an ashen face gritted his teeth against the pain of a broken leg.

The wagon pulled to a stop as the sheriff and his deputy stepped to the edge of the roadway. The cowboys stared defiantly at the

12

two peace officers. No one spoke for a moment. Obie Grant broke the silence.

"It looks," he said quietly, "like you Cross-J hombres have been playing rough again — and mebbe got the worst of it this time. Mebbe you'd better drop the 'cross' part outten your brand."

"Don't jump to any conclusions, Obie," the hard-eyed man next to the driver snapped. "This is just the first load. Wait until you see the contribution them fool hoe men bring in. The undertaker is going to be plumb swamped with business —"

"You, Brazos," the sheriff interrupted, "when you and your outfit going to stop this damn foolishness?"

Brazos Burnett shifted his lean, whipcord length to bend down and tap the sheriff on the chest. "We ain't stopping until these damn nesters quit stringing wire, Zach. It's up to them to get out. We won't never leave. And" — his grizzled features hardened — "I reckon we can dish out just a mite more than they can take."

The sheriff sighed. "You're bucking the law, Brazos."

"Alex Jenkins don't see it that way," Brazos said coldly. "I'm taking orders from Alex. We don't ask you to side with us, Zach. All's we ask is for you to keep hands off."

"Maybe I can't do that any longer," the sheriff said. "Maybe the time's come for me

13

to take sides, whether I like it or not." His gaze shifted uncomfortably. "I got a duty —"

"That," Brazos cut in coldly, "is up to you, Zach. *Our* way is clear, as we see it. You know what we're fighting, whether you admit it or not. That's Bob Preuss laying under that blanket in this wagon. He called himself a friend of yours."

The sheriff swallowed hard and cast a reluctant eye at the cold form stretched stiffly beneath the blanket. "That's bad news to me, but" — uncomfortably — "he was cutting wire when it happened, wa'n't he?"

"And doing a damn good job of it," Brazos snapped. "Think over who put that wire there. Bob Preuss was loyal to his friends."

"Meaning I'm not, I suppose." Robertson sighed.

"That's for you to decide, Zach."

Deputy Grant put in mildly, "You hombres are putting it to Zach the hard way. He's trying to be fair. The fact remains the Cross-J is breaking the law every time it snips wire —"

"A hell of a law!" a hard-faced puncher spat.

Obie eyed the man steadily. "It could be enforced, you know."

"You aimin' to try it?" the puncher challenged.

"I'd sure like to," Obie assured the man.

14

The sheriff raised a protesting hand. "Leave be, Obie."

Brazos said, "That goes for you too, Yank. Me and Zach will do the talking."

The sheriff changed the subject: "Where's Alex? How come he didn't come in with y'all?"

"Alex," Brazos told him with cold humor, "got took with a mite of lead poisoning in one arm. We're taking the doctor back with us —"

"Serious?" the sheriff asked quickly.

"Not none," Brazos said. The sheriff looked relieved. He glanced at the grim features staring down at him from the driver's seat and from the backs of horses. They were dust-covered, powder-grimed, relentlessly hard, determined. Maybe there was a certain amount of contempt there too. The sheriff wasn't certain. Of one thing he was sure: the Cross-J felt they were in the right, and they weren't fearful of anything he might do. It gradually dawned on him that these men, only recently firm friends, were swiftly assuming the appearance of belligerent strangers.

The cowboy with the broken leg, stretched next to the dead man, spoke through clenched teeth: "We goin' to stay here jawin' all day, Brazos? I'd sure like to get to Doc Kilburn's."

The punchers were suddenly full of concern, regrets. Brazos nodded stiffly to the sheriff and his deputy. The wagon rolled on, stirring the thick dust in the road, and turned left at the next corner. The sheriff looked after them a few moments, then said, "It's hell when you have to have a bodyguard to bring in your wounded and dead."

Obie agreed. "But those nesters wouldn't overlook any opportunities, if only one came in with the wagon. . . . I wonder when the other side will put in an appearance — not that I think there'll be a ruckus in town, should the trails of the two factions cross. You've been firm enough on that end, Zach, and they've respected your wishes."

The Cross-J wagon and riders left town an hour later without again stopping before the sheriff's. By this time the town was well astir. When the other faction finally did put in an appearance it drove directly to the undertaker's. There weren't any wounded men to be taken to the doctor's. Swearing nervously, the sheriff jammed on his sombrero and hastened after the wagon. Half an hour later he returned slowly to his office. Obie was seated on the porch, chair tilted back against the front wall. The sheriff looked harassed; he was perspiring profusely.

Obie asked, "What did you learn?"

The sheriff swallowed hard. "Ben Cassidy was there when I arrived. He's insisting that I throw the whole Cross-J outfit under arrest.

16

His language was right mean. Five nesters — if you want to call 'em that — were rubbed out last night. Cassidy'll make trouble. He like to wore me down with his demands."

"You look sort of whupped. Me, I don't like Cassidy none, but I got to admit he's within his legal rights. You going to make them arrests?"

"I'll be damned if I will!" Robertson exploded. "Obie, I got my mind made up. I'm going to telegraph the governor to send soldiers here to handle this business."

"Soldiers?" Obie looked aghast. "Soldiers! Cripes a'mighty, Zach! That's admitting the situation is beyond your control. Look! You can't do that —"

"Maybe it is beyond my control," the sheriff said doggedly. "I'd resign from office, only the next man might not see things the way I do. I won't do anything to hurt Alex Jenkins. A small detachment of cavalry could handle this whole business and bring peace. This killing has got to stop."

"Zach," Obie protested, "not soldiers! Your mind ain't thinking straight."

"Maybe it ain't," the sheriff said nervously. "I ain't sure, myself. That's why I figure to throw the whole responsibility on the governor's shoulders. In that way I won't have to act, personal, against the Cross-J."

Obie said unbelievingly, "And you think by calling the soldiers here you won't be acting against the Cross-J? Don't you know it'll take more than a uniform to scare Alex Jenkins? Hell, Zach, you're just dodging the issue. Think this over a spell before you do anything crazy."

"Think!" the sheriff exclaimed wildly. "I ain't done nothing else but think — and I don't want no more arguments."

Obie shrugged his bony shoulders. "You're the boss," he said quietly. "I'll go saddle up while you're writing out your message for the governor."

"Saddle my horse, Obie. I'll make the ride to Fritada myself with the telegram."

"It's going to be a hot day, Zach. There's no need of you making that ride to the depot —"

"There's a hell of a lot more need than you think," the sheriff snapped testily. "If I can't get away from Painted Post and the sound of guns and the smell of death for a spell, I'll go crazy." His tones dropped to normal. He looked a bit ashamed of himself and very old. "Maybe a ride will do me good; maybe, come evening, I'll cool down."

Obie didn't say anything more. He looked queerly at his superior, then stepped from the porch and headed for the corral out back. The sheriff pressed one hand against his forehead and walked slowly to the pine desk inside his office. His fingers were shaking as he commenced putting words on a sheet of paper.

II. "Ride 'Em, Ranger!"

Johnny Auburn's high-heeled boots made clumping sounds on the boardwalk as he strode along East Crockett Street in San Antonio, heading in the direction of a small rock house situated not a great distance from the historic Alamo. Johnny was lean and straight and muscular-jawed. His well-worn sombrero was thrust jauntily back on his head of flame-colored hair. He had gray eyes and an infectious smile. There was a cartridge belt strapped about his slim hips, from which was suspended a holstered forty-five six-shooter. He wore a woolen shirt with knotted bandanna at the throat, corduroy trousers tucked into boot tops, and a stringy vest. He whistled as he walked, and one hand jingled some coins in a trousers' pocket.

Arriving at his destination, he knocked lightly on the jamb of the open door set flush with the sidewalk and hesitated a moment. Within the building a keen-eyed man of about thirty-five years raised his head from the papers he'd been studying on a table before him and said, "Come on in. Oh, it's you, Johnny."

Johnny stood stiffly at the table. "You sent for me, Captain Travis?"

George Travis, Captain, Company K, Texas Rangers, smiled slightly. His clothing was very similar to that of Johnny's. "Relax," he ordered. "Forget the formalities and find a chair. Were you doing anything special? Hope I didn't interrupt."

Johnny drew up a chair and sat down on the opposite side of the long table. "Nothing too special, sir. I'd just looked into the Elephant — y'know, over on Main Plaza — for a short spell." He grinned suddenly and jingled the gold coins in his pocket. "I'd just decided to pull out when the Mex kid came with your note."

Travis smiled. "The cards must have been running your way, Johnny."

"They sure weren't ignoring me that I could see." Johnny's voice was soft and drawly. "But I'm interrupting. What is it, sir? Are we going into camp, back to Bandera?"

"Growing tired of town already?"

"I like open country best. Fact of the matter is, Captain, I've been thinking of resigning. I'd like to go back to beef raising — get an outfit of my own."

Travis nodded sober comprehension. "I think I know how you feel. I'd hate to see you leave the Rangers, though. You'll be in line for a captaincy one of these days, but then I don't reckon you'll ever save enough for an outfit on Ranger's pay. In a way it's a tough life, Johnny."

"It has its compensations. I'm satisfied. And I'm not figuring on buying my spread on Ranger's pay." He grinned again and jingled the coins in his pocket. "I sure enough been lucky."

"That's good." Travis changed the subject: "I've got a job for you, Johnny, one that has certain queer angles. I'm not even sure what the setup is. It's up to you to find out — and settle it peacefully —"

"Meaning," Johnny put in dryly, "the Rangers' kind of peace?"

"Exactly." Travis nodded. "If there's any shooting done, I want you to be the one to do the talking afterward."

Johnny asked, "What is it — rustling, bank robbery, a murder?"

"None of the three. Fence cutting."

"Fence cutting?" Johnny looked surprised. "I thought we had that game all cleaned up some spell back. Same old story, I suppose: some big wolf gobbling the holdings of the sheep — and the sheep are putting up a yelp."

Travis shook his head. "No, this time it's the sheep fencing off the big cattleman. It's the big man cutting the fences. There's been a lot of shooting — and killing — on both sides."

Johnny frowned. "When the little men

21

jump the big owner that puts a new angle on the business. I'm interested. You don't mean sheepmen are moving in on a stockman?"

"I was only using your own figure of speech when I mentioned sheep. The sheep in this case are farmers — maybe nesters. Leastwise, Jenkins claims they're nesters. I've a hunch he's wrong. You ever been up in the Painted Post country?"

"Never have. I know it's up in Painted Post County, up in the north part of the state. Don't know much about it."

Travis nodded. "The county seat is called Painted Post too. It's sort of out of the way; the railroad cut south of Painted Post, and there aren't too many folks get up that way. Sort of desert country at many spots, but there are some damn nice valleys at others. Here's the story as I get it. There's a cowman up there named Jenkins who raises a heap of cattle. I don't know how many years he's been in there — maybe he doesn't either. Anyway, it's always been open range up there and he never bothered to record his land in any way —"

"And so it's open to settlement," Johnny put in.

"Right. Not only open, but in process of being settled, if the farmers have their way. They've leased sections from the state and went in there, as they have a right to do, and started to put up fences. As fast as they go up, Jenkins — he brands a Cross-J — cuts the wire. Hence the shooting and killing."

"Sounds simple to me. When a man leases a piece of land he has a right to fence it, regardless who's been running cattle there. We can get out an injunction to stop the fence cutting. Then if Jenkins doesn't want to obey the law he can be arrested. This Jenkins sounds like a cantankerous old coot to me. Maybe a few hours in the cooler will change his tune."

Travis said dryly, "You turning against the cowman in favor of the nester?"

Johnny flushed. "I wasn't speaking my own mind on the subject. I was just stating what the law says is right. I'm sworn to enforce the law. I'm stating what can be done — under the law. I still think the cattleman deserves a better break than he gets sometimes."

"Apparently that's what the sheriff of Painted Post thinks too. Feller name of Robertson. He refuses, himself, to take sides. Instead, he wired the governor to send soldiers there to settle the problem. I don't know if Robertson lost his nerve or what. Anyway, I had this long telegram from the governor this morning" — pointing to several sheets on the table — "in which he outlined as much of the story as he could give me. He asks that I send a Ranger up to look over the situation."

Johnny grinned suddenly. "I'll bet that

would burn the Army if they knew it. The sheriff requests troops and the governor figures one Ranger is equal to the troops."

Travis smiled. "Governor Ireland is a close personal friend. I'd like to help him get this matter straightened out. But I haven't told you all of it. The day following the receipt of the wire from the sheriff, the governor received another wire from the deputy sheriff, stating that he didn't think soldiers were necessary. How do you figure that?"

"Looks like the deputy and his boss aren't agreed on the subject. Maybe the deputy is doing some double-crossing. Is the deputy working with the nesters — or land leasers, or whatever you want to call 'em?"

"I don't know. It's up to you to find out."

"How many farmers have moved in up there?"

"About fifty, I understand. And they apparently know how to handle guns as well as hoes."

"All arrive at once, or did they filter in gradually?"

"They arrived over a period of a couple of weeks, I think."

"Who's heading 'em?"

"What do you mean, who is heading them?" Travis frowned.

Johnny explained: "Any crowd that arrives that close together must be organized. There's a head to every organization. There must be in this case. Who is he?"

"I can't say that I know," Travis replied, "unless it's a man named Ben Cassidy, who is, from all the governor says, pressing for the action that Sheriff Robertson refuses to give — personally."

"This Robertson don't seem to be thinking straight; his firing pin seems to be striking off center — Wait a minute! Ben Cassidy, you say? Just a second while I give a look."

Johnny Auburn reached to a pocket and whipped out a black leather-covered notebook that showed considerable wear.

Travis smiled. "You and your portable file of suspects." He chuckled good-naturedly. "Well, it's come in mighty handy on other occasions, but don't tell me you've got Ben Cassidy down in it."

"Yes sir, I believe I have." Johnny riffled the pages swiftly. "Maybe this isn't the same man, but here's the name: Cassidy, Benjamin; murder; acquitted." Johnny's forehead wrinkled into a furrow of thought for a moment. "I remember now, sir. It happened in Santa Angela. It was right after the flood wiped out that town of Ben Ficklin. The survivors moved to Over-the-River and changed the name to Santa Angela — just a few years back."

"Damn if you aren't a walking encyclopedia." Travis smiled. "I remember now. You went up there to check into a robbery that took place while the flood was on. But

Cassidy had nothing to do with that —"

"No sir. Cassidy got in a scrape over a card game in Santa Angela. He was caught cheating and pulled a gun on his accuser, but the other feller held the draw and ran Cassidy out. They met two or three times after that. When Cassidy got the chance he plugged the feller in the back. Trouble was, Cassidy had a lot of friends as witnesses. They swore that Cassidy had to kill or be killed. It was a dirty deal, and Cassidy was acquitted. I was planning to do something about it, but Cassidy skipped out for Las Vegas before I could stop him. . . . I wonder if this is the same Cassidy. Maybe Sheriff Robertson isn't so crazy after all, if he's bucking the Cassidy I knew —"

Travis broke in: "You seem to take it to heart, Johnny. After all, you couldn't have done anything about Cassidy, once he was acquitted."

"I realize that, sir. But I figured I could maybe get him on something else. Captain! I want to go up to Painted Post and look into this."

Travis chuckled. "I've already told you you're picked for the job. If you can gather your things you can leave within the hour. Take your saddle and other duffel you need." He consulted a heavy gold watch. "You can catch the train to Fort Worth in exactly fifty-eight minutes. I've already figured out your

26

trip, you see. At Fort Worth you change to the Texas & Pacific Railroad as far as a town called Fritada. That'll drop you in the middle of some desert country — just a small Mex town there. You'll have to pick up a horse there too — either that or walk the fifteen miles north to Painted Post."

"I can be ready inside twenty minutes, sir — if not less."

"Good! I'll walk over to your quarters with you and we'll have time to stop at the Menger for a cold beer. And when you get to Painted Post, if you find anything crooked going on, go after the crooks, Ranger. Ride 'em and ride 'em hard! Clean up this business as soon as possible. Regardless of how the situation shapes up, enforce the law. I've got a hunch you may find your sympathies siding with the cow folks. That must not make the slightest difference. I'm sending a telegram to Governor Ireland today, to let him know I've put you on the job. Then he can inform Sheriff Robertson you're coming. But I want you to rigidly enforce the law. Will you promise me that?"

"I promise, sir."

"And wire me at once, as soon as you've settled the business."

"I'll do that."

"Fine." Captain Travis rose and got his sombrero. "Come on. If we hurry we may have time for two cold bottles."

III. Cassidy Thinks Fast

Of the two men seated in the Maverick Saloon, one was its proprietor, Cold-Deck Malotte. Cold-Deck was thin to the point of emaciation; his face was lined and hard, making him look ten years older than his present age of thirty-five. Cold-Deck had aspired to be a gambling man of the more deft variety, but a certain clumsiness in his manipulations had so often led to exposure — with the consequent hasty leaving of his seat of operations — that by the time he'd arrived in Painted Post, where he wasn't known, he had come to the conclusion that, perhaps, the sale of liquor was more in his line. He still looked the part of the professional gambler, however, and still plied his nefarious trade when he could draw some greenhorn into his web. His very name, however, warned off the less stupid of his prospective victims, even though he had tried to laugh off the "Cold-Deck" a few years previously, when it had first been applied to him by Brazos Burnett, foreman of the Cross-J outfit. But somehow the name had stuck — or Malotte was stuck with it, to be more exact.

Seated on the opposite side of the round, wooden-topped table was Tascosa Jake Wiley. Tascosa was of medium height, with a week's crop of whiskers on his weathered countenance and a pair of closely set pale blue eyes. To those who knew him, Tascosa carried a reputation as a killer. There were notches in the walnut butts of the twin Colt guns carried at his hips, though, so far as anyone knew, none of those notches had been carved since his arrival in Painted Post. He wore cowman's boots, dark trousers with a thin gray stripe in them, and a checkered woolen shirt. A ragged-brimmed sombrero covered his tousled clay-colored hair. Even when he had money Tascosa wore that same old battered hat.

The two men were talking in low tones, heads close together over the table top. After a time Cold-Deck reached to his glass and saw it was empty. He turned in his chair and called across the barroom to his bartender behind the long counter: "Louie, bring a bottle over here. Better bring another glass too. Ben will be coming along, I expect."

Louis, a slick-haired individual with a slack jaw, brought the bottle and empty glass. There weren't any other men in the saloon. Cold-Deck motioned Louie away, filled his own and Tascosa's glasses, gulped off the fiery liquor, then leaned back in his chair.

"So you see," he said, "that's the way it will work out."

Tascosa's pale blue eyes had a dubious light in them. "I don't know," he said slowly. "Maybe it will; maybe it won't. I don't take to this idea of getting soldiers here. Ain't no bunch of fancy uniforms going to make Alex Jenkins back down — not a cantankerous coot like him. He'll just go on the prod all the harder, the way I see it."

"Exactly." Cold-Deck smiled thinly. "That's what Ben had in mind. He hinted around about soldiers until the sheriff fell for the idea, thinking he'd thought of it himself. The soldiers will come here. Like you say, Jenkins will really go on the warpath then. That will be the end of the Cross-J. Did you ever hear of anybody bucking the soldiers? I never did. Ben's smart, I tell you. The way he's worked out things, the soldiers do our fighting for us. We don't risk a hair."

Tascosa spat a long brown stream on the worn floorboards. "Me, I don't mind risking a hair," he growled.

Cold-Deck started to reply, then thought better of it. He stretched back in his chair and stared meditatively through the open door of the saloon, where the hot noon sunlight picked out dust motes in the still air. Finally he said, "That's how you look at it. It was me put this whole thing up to Ben and brought him here. I figure he's got the brain to see it through. That makes us two against you. Anyway, it's done and we can't change

30

it — Wait! Here's Ben now."

A shadow darkened the doorway, and Ben Cassidy entered the saloon. He was a tall, well-built individual, with dark hair and eyes. His lips were thin and straight; on the upper one was a closely shaven black mustache. He wore a fancy vest but no coat. His shirt was white and held at the collar by a knotted black string tie. His trousers were gray, tucked into boot tops; a cartridge belt and holstered forty-five hung at his right thigh. He was smoking a long thin cigar as he strode in and settled himself on a straight-backed chair between the two men.

Tascosa started to speak, then noted that his boss's brow was furrowed deeply with thought. Cold-Deck poured whisky into the waiting glass and shoved it toward Cassidy. Cassidy picked up the glass, studied it a moment, then downed the contents. He placed the glass back on the table, brushed his lips with a bandanna handkerchief, and eyed the other two with a somewhat wry smile.

Cold-Deck said impatiently, "Well, has Robertson had an answer to his telegram yet?"

"A Mex brought it from Fritada about twenty minutes ago." Cassidy nodded.

"Soldiers coming, eh?" Tascosa growled.

Cassidy shook his head. "It didn't work out quite like I figured. Instead of sending troops, the governor is sending a Texas Ranger here."

31

Cold-Deck swore suddenly. Cassidy looked at him and nodded agreement to the thought in Cold-Deck's mind. "I don't like it either," he told Malotte. "I've got to do some fast thinking."

Tascosa brightened. "I always did have a hankering to cross guns with a Ranger."

"You're a damned fool," Cassidy told him bluntly. "Rangers are poison. We could have pulled the wool over the soldiers' eyes, without much trouble, but — well, I just don't like Rangers. Look, Tascosa, until you hit Texas you'd never been anywhere but around Kansas and Oklahoma. Sure, I know, you made yourself a rep when you landed in Tascosa, when that cowboy strike was on. And you hired your guns to the rancher element —"

"I done my share to break that strike," Tascosa put in. "I got two notches that says so." He turned indignantly to Cold-Deck. "Can you imagine the nerve of them cow hands — saving their wages and then giving the owners notice they wouldn't herd no more stock unless they got higher pay? We busted that idea higher'n a kite —"

"All right, all right," Cassidy interrupted testily. "So you worked yourself up a rep as a tough hombre. Yes, I know, you even claim you made Pat Garrett back down once too. Maybe you did. I wasn't there."

"You doubting my word?" Tascosa demanded belligerently.

"I'm not even giving it any thought one way or the other," Cassidy said flatly. "The point I'm making is just this: you may be a rootin'-tootin' son, but you've never yet bucked a Ranger. They're bad medicine on lawbreakers. You just don't know 'em."

"I've heard of 'em," Tascosa growled. "Sure, they've done a lot of law-enforcing down south, along the border, where they shot up Mexes and Injuns. All I asks is a chance at one of 'em."

"Maybe you'll get it sooner than you hope," Cassidy snapped. "But I'm going to try something else first. If possible I'd like to stop that Ranger ever getting here."

"What's the use?" Cold-Deck asked. "They'd just send another — and another. Those hombres don't give up. Geez! How I hate the bustards."

"You listen to me," Cassidy said. "I've talked to the sheriff about this. I've got him thinking he don't want a Ranger here either. I've told him he asked for soldiers and he's entitled to soldiers. Got him to thinking that was his own idea." Cassidy smiled thinly. "The poor fool is so nervous that he don't know whether he's coming or going." He drew deeply on his cigar and sent a cloud of gray smoke floating around the room. "I kind of got a hunch he'll ride out to head that Ranger off. If something was to happen to both him and the Ranger and it could be made to look like they'd had a fight and shot it out — well, do you see what I mean?"

"I don't know as I do." Cold-Deck frowned. "You get rid of the sheriff and the Ranger and you throw all the law enforcement in Obie Grant's hands. He won't fool so easy as Robertson."

"We can take care of Grant the same way, can't we?" Cassidy asked coldly. "From then on we run things to suit ourselves. The Cross-J won't yell for law enforcement. Alex Jenkins don't want any law officers cutting in on the game. So we'll have a clear field."

"Just how you figuring to work all this?" Tascosa asked.

"I'll tell you in just a minute. Cold-Deck, send Louie out to find Mitch Bailey. I want to tell him we've got a job for his scatter-gun." Cold-Deck sent the bartender on the errand. "Now, pour me another drink," Cassidy continued, "and I'll get down to cases. Maybe the Rangers never yet been stopped in Texas, but there's always a first time. I figure we're due to do the stopping!" He lifted his glass. "Here's to death for a Ranger!"

IV. Shotgun Barrier

It was shortly after one in the afternoon when Johnny Auburn stepped down from the train that had carried him to Fritada. In one hand he carried a small valise containing personal belongings; from the other swung his saddle. There hadn't been any other passengers destined for Fritada. Smoke and steam billowed and swirled about Johnny, then vanished in the clear, sunbaked air as the train thundered rapidly down the track. Johnny looked about him.

The railroad depot was a frame shack painted a bright red, with a wide apron of crushed cinders around it. In one open doorway stood the station agent, a man about thirty years of age, wearing bibbed overalls and a derby hat. The man looked Johnny over uncompromisingly and spat. Then he said, "I reckon you're the Ranger man that's due here."

Johnny grinned. "According to this badge I'm wearing, I am. You heard about me, eh?"

"It was me that sent Sheriff Robertson's message to the governor, and it was me who took the reply. I sent it out, pronto, to the sheriff yesterday. Kind of thought you might get here last night."

Johnny shook his head. "I missed the Limited, due to my train to Fort Worth being delayed. I understand there's a mite of promiscuous lead being tossed around over beyond Painted Post."

"No matter what name you put to it, it kills just like any other lead. You aiming to step on Alex Jenkins any?"

Johnny said quietly, "I haven't decided yet what I'll do until I look over the situation. I'll enforce the law; I know that much."

The station agent spat and said, "Alex Jenkins is all right. I can't say as much for Cassidy and his gang. Some went to Painted Post by wagon, but a heap of 'em landed here first. Maybe they're farmers — I won't say they're not — but I'm betting they'll raise more hell than crops. Just so long as you give Alex a square deal, that's all I ask. My name's John Cummings."

"I'm John too — only they call me Johnny — Johnny Auburn. And I need a horse."

"Figured you might. I got one for you. Best little horse in Fritada. A Mex owned him, but he owed me some money. I arranged yesterday to take the horse instead. I got him tied t'other side of the depot. Give him a look and then we'll dicker."

Johnny dropped his valise and, carrying the saddle, rounded the building to see a well-set-up, buckskin gelding with a cream-colored mane and tail. Johnny saddled up and got aboard after slipping off the hackamore that held the pony to a corner of the depot. The buckskin went high in the air, came down, rose again; it gave a few short, jerky bucks, then stood quiet.

"I think you'll do, pony," Johnny said quietly and rode around to confront Cummings again. "John," he said, "you've sold a horse for forty dollars."

The station agent grunted. "Mebbe so — but not that horse. His price is sixty. What's wrong with him?"

Johnny chuckled. "Pretty nigh everything. I suspect glanders, stringhalt, botflies, thrush — Subject to colic, too, isn't he? 'Bout twenty years old, I figure, from the looks of his teeth. Only that I need a horse bad, I wouldn't even look at him."

"That little pony is sound as a dollar, and you know it. The price is sixty bucks. He'll travel night and day, go without water and feed, if necessary. He'll run his heart out for you. And he's only a three-year-old. I've seen him win races —"

"I'll give you forty-five dollars."

"— more than once," the stationman flowed on. "If I told you his time for a mile you'd never believe it. He can be taught tricks, just like a dog. He'll fight Injuns at the drop of the hat, or tend little babies just like a nurse would do. He don't muss up a bed, and his table manners is neat, and I wouldn't take less than fifty-five —"

"By the look in his eye he's a killer," Johnny interrupted gravely. "A genuine outlaw. I'd be taking my life in my hands every time I stepped on him —"

"— for a sweet little horse that you could bed down in his saddle, and he'd never disturb your sleep. He'll fetch and carry, cook meals, make up bunks, shoe hisself when necessary, and my final price is —"

"Fifty bucks flat," Johnny cut in, "providing he can fiddle to a square dance and catch fish — No, no, wait! I won't go a cent higher, even if he can darn socks."

"Fifty it is," the station agent accepted, realizing Johnny had said the last word. He was satisfied. They had struck a happy medium between the first price asked and the first price offered. "I'm just sort of sorry you're taking him, though. I was teaching him to run that telegram machine of mine. I'll write you a bill of sale. His name is Cherokee."

Johnny paid over the money and received his bill of sale. Lashing the valise to the saddle, he again climbed up and prepared to depart. "Just as a matter of curiosity," he said gravely, "I'm wondering how much was owed you by the Mex whose horse you took in place of the debt."

Cummings suddenly laughed. "Eight dollars and four bits."

Johnny said dryly, "I always heard there was money in railroading."

"There is — but not every day. Only that you're named John, same as me, I don't think I'd have let you have that little horse."

"I don't doubt it," Johnny agreed. "You'll probably miss having him around to cook your meals and sweep out the station. So long, John." He shifted his gun a trifle and moved on.

"So long, Johnny. And give Alex Jenkins a square deal."

Johnny left the station and cut through the main street of Fritada which was made up of a collection of adobe huts and small frame shacks. There were a lot of Mexicans siestaing in the shadows between buildings. It wasn't much of a town, but with the railroad coming through, it would undoubtedly boom in time.

Leaving the town behind, Johnny headed north in open country. All about was a sort of semidesert terrain. There were some prickly pear here and there and scattered clumps of scrubby mesquite. Off to the left a mile or so a wide salt sink gleamed dazzlingly white in the sunlight. Ahead, hazy in the distance, rose a long, rolling hill horizon. There'd be trees there and grass. It would be cooler too. Johnny spoke to the buckskin pony, and it lifted its gait in response. "Cherokee," Johnny said, "I think you and me are going to be pals, and I'll bet I got a bargain, even if your price was high." The horse pricked its ears understandingly and loped on.

Gradually Johnny found himself getting into rolling hill country. The grass that had been sparse a few miles back became thicker; the mesquite trees grew taller; here and there he spotted small stands of post oak. The Painted Post Mountains were no longer hazy on his left. He could see the lower slopes covered with timber. On his right the first foothills of the Little Painted Post Range commenced to appear; he was approaching the long valley in which was situated the Cross-J range. There was more rock to be seen now, too, along the well-defined trail that ran to Painted Post.

The way dipped to pass between two giant sandstone rock piles. The huge boulders rose on either side of Johnny, cutting off his view of the open range. A few yards ahead the trail curved sharply. And then, as Johnny rounded the curve, he abruptly drew rein.

Blocking his way sat a horseman holding a double-barreled shotgun that pointed directly at Johnny. The man who barred his way was ugly-visaged, bewhiskered, dirty. Johnny spoke first, dryly: "What is this, a surprise party?"

"That's what it's meant to be, Ranger

40

Man," the fellow growled. He tilted the shot-gun a trifle. "You ain't goin' no further."

"Meaning," Johnny asked softly, "I'm sup-posed to turn back?"

"That ain't the idea, neither, Ranger Man. You're stoppin' here — now!"

Johnny saw it coming, read the murderous intent in the man's eyes, sensed the tighter curving of fingers about the shotgun's trig-gers. The gun was so close he could almost have reached out and seized it but didn't dare risk that.

"Now, look here, feller," Johnny com-menced in a placating tone. Then he acted, plunging his spurs sharply against Cherokee's ribs; at the same instant his right hand darted toward his holster. Startled, the buck-skin horse leaped suddenly forward, crashing into the other pony and causing it to rear.

There came the double, heavy report of the shotgun, with the loads flying wildly over Johnny's head. Johnny fired even as his pony moved in. He saw his adversary sway in the saddle, the shotgun dropping from nerveless hands. A second shot left Johnny's gun even before the fellow struck the gravelly earth.

The riderless horse neighed with terror, whirled on hind hoofs, and went clattering off, headed in the direction of Painted Post. Johnny looked at its rider sprawled on the ground a few yards away. The man lay quite still on his face, blood already commencing

41

to seep into the earth beneath the body. Johnny patted the quivering buckskin to still its nervousness, then stepped carefully down. The buckskin stood quiet. "You sure got me out of that mess, pony," Johnny said softly.

He stooped over the man on the ground, turned him over. The fellow was quite dead. Methodically Johnny went through his pockets. They produced a couple of letters addressed to "Mitch Bailey," a half-consumed plug of chewing tobacco, a small knife, and other odds and ends. Aside from the shotgun, Bailey hadn't been armed; he didn't carry a six-shooter. Johnny straightened up, reloading his depleted forty-five chambers.

He had started to get back into his saddle when something caught his eye. A booted toe showed from behind a big boulder about thirty feet away. Johnny stepped swiftly to the spot and there found a second dead man, this one wearing, on his open vest, a sheriff's star of office. A quick examination showed the dead sheriff had been shot twice through the middle, with, Johnny judged, a six-shooter. Near by lay a second shotgun. Johnny "broke" it and discovered two exploded shells.

"They're sure hell on scatter-guns in this country," he mused, closing the gun again. His gaze returned to the dead man. "I wonder if you're Sheriff Robertson — and who killed you? That hombre that tried to stop me didn't tote a six-shooter. This is one queer mix-up. How'd you get here? I don't see your horse. Maybe it ran off like the other one."

White clouds drifted overhead. Johnny set about scrutinizing the earth in search of "sign" that might furnish a clue to the mystery. He worked slowly in a northerly direction for some fifty yards before his keen eyes caught the glint of two empty forty-five shells on the sand. There were footprints here, too, as well as hoofmarks. The horses had moved off in the direction of Painted Post. Johnny guessed that someone had led a riderless horse.

Finally, after Johnny had learned as much as seemed possible, he slowly retraced his steps to the buckskin pony, cast a last look at the dead Mitch Bailey, and climbed into the saddle.

"Cherokee," he said, "I don't know how you're going to like it, but you're due to carry double the rest of this journey. There's a dead sheriff yonderly. We've got to tote him in. Let's get going, pony."

V. Johnny Goes Down

The sun was dropping behind the cedar-covered hills when Johnny and Deputy Obie Grant emerged from the undertaker's place of business in Painted Post. "And there," Obie observed, hard-eyed, "is the last of Zach Robertson. If I could only learn who killed him. . . ." He paused, clenching his fists, then gulped hard: "I thought a heap of Zach."

They moved out to the street where the buckskin horse was waiting. Johnny picked up the reins and led the horse behind him as the two men turned the corner on Painted Post's main thoroughfare which was known as Chisholm Street. Along Chisholm there was an almost unbroken line of hitch racks. Several pedestrians negotiated the plank sidewalks. As they walked on Johnny observed three or four saloons, a general store, a small bank, and a building proclaiming, by its weather-beaten sign, that it was the Painted Post Hotel.

Obie was talking again: "One thing I'm wondering about, where do I stand now, Auburn? Am I still a deputy, with you here, or — ?"

"You'll act as sheriff for the present," Johnny replied, "at least until I leave, or the authorities make some other arrangement. . . . You're sure that was the sheriff's shotgun I brought in?"

"Hell, yes. I'd know it anywhere. I should have pointed out to you where Zach scratched his initials on the butt a few months back. You say both shells were exploded when you found it?"

Johnny nodded. "When they were fired, I don't know, of course. I figure the sheriff had been dead about two hours before I got there. The sand where his blood had dripped was still dampish. The way I figure from the sign, two men went out and waited for the sheriff. One of 'em was this Mitch Bailey, but he didn't kill Robertson. He didn't have a six-shooter. It was the other man did the job. Then he left, leading the sheriff's horse, and eventually turned the beast loose."

Obie said, "Yeah, Zach's horse wandered in about an hour before you brought in the body." He sighed. "Maybe it's just as well Zach went like he did. He's been nearly crazy the past several weeks, trying to do what was right. His health ain't been good the past year, neither. He went to Fort Worth a couple of times to see doctors, but they couldn't hold out much hope. Zach told me once he only figured he'd live a couple of years more. He had some sort of growth in

45

his stomach. That added to his worry. Had he been able to think straight, I know he'd never have sent for soldiers. That was why I sent that other telegram telling the governor soldiers wa'n't necessary. Cripes! I told you all this before. But you can see I was trying to make things look as good for Zach as possible." Obie's eyes looked misty in the light from the setting sun.

"Sure, Obie, sure, I understand," Johnny said quietly. "The sheriff knew his duty but just couldn't bring himself to act against the Cross-J. In a way, from what you've told me about the Cassidy crowd, I can see his viewpoint, and yet the law's the law. I'll be glad to lay eyes on this Cassidy hombre if and when he comes to town."

"He's shying off," Obie said bitterly. "I heard him talking to the sheriff, prodding him on, telling him to insist on soldiers and to stop a Ranger coming here. Zach was nigh out of his head. He rode out last night to meet you on the way, to try to persuade you to turn back. Then when you didn't show up he rode out again this morning. I told him it wouldn't do any good, but he wouldn't listen to reason. It was last night he noticed his shotgun wasn't on its regular rack. He thought I'd taken it. Somebody slipped into the office while I was out and lifted it, I suppose. But why, why?"

"That's something we'll have to find out,"

46

Johnny said patiently. "I want to see Cassidy, then I'll drift out to the Cross-J and talk to Alex Jenkins."

"You'll find him a cantankerous coot, but square —"

"He's been breaking the law," Johnny pointed out.

"Law or no law," Obie said bitterly, "I'm betting you'll like him better than this scum Cassidy has brought in. And then you'll find yourself in the same position Zach was — between two fires. You being a Ranger won't scare Jenkins any. There's plenty trouble ahead, Johnny Auburn."

Johnny said simply, "We'll meet it when it comes."

"You'll have the whole cowman faction against you if you take up for Cassidy. I'm just glad it's you and not me."

"I may have to call on you for help."

"I'll give it, even if it goes against the grain. I've sworn to do my duty — though I got a good notion to resign —"

"You can't resign while things are this way."

Obie didn't reply. They walked on, booted feet scuffing through the dust, the buckskin moving easily behind. As they neared the sheriff's office Obie pointed out the livery stable which stood directly across the street. Johnny took the pony across and after giving directions relative to feeding and rubbing

47

down picked up his valise and returned to the sheriff's office.

Obie was just lighting an oil lamp on the desk when Johnny stepped in. He was through the door before he noticed that Obie had a visitor, a slim, dark-eyed girl with tanned skin and a firm mouth. She wore riding boots, a divided riding skirt, mannish flannel shirt, and a fawn-colored sombrero.

"Yes, Miss Pat, it's true," Obie was saying heavily. "The sheriff's body was brought in just a spell ago by Johnny Auburn, the Ranger I mentioned — Oh, hello, Johnny! Johnny, this is Miss Patricia Jenkins. Her paw owns the Cross-J spread. This is Mister Auburn, Miss Pat."

The girl eyed Johnny coldly. She made no effort to put out her hand. Johnny said, "I'm glad to meet you, miss," and removed his sombrero. He placed his valise on the floor.

The girl said bitterly, "I doubt the Cross-J will have similar sentiments."

Johnny's lips twitched slightly. "That," he announced, "is plumb likely to break me all up."

The girl flushed. "That won't hurt anybody's feelings on the Cross-J."

Johnny laughed softly. "You're frank, anyway."

"Why shouldn't I be?" Pat Jenkins demanded hotly. "You're here to try and enforce the law against us. You're taking the side of Ben Cassidy and his gang —"

"Miss Jenkins," Johnny said quietly, "I haven't taken sides with anybody yet. I'll act when I learn how things stand. Meanwhile, a murder was committed today. I want to find that murderer. If you'd let me, I'd like to be friends."

"I'm afraid," the girl said in chilly accents, "that is impossible." She nodded to Johnny, said good night to Obie, and strode angrily through the doorway. Johnny looked after her in admiration.

"There," he states emphatically, "goes one pretty girl."

"Pat's all right," Obie agreed somberly, "but I don't think you and her are ever going to get along. She's got spirit, just like old Alex. You start bucking her old man and you got to take her into consideration as well. She ain't namby-pamby."

"What's she doing here?"

"Her and some of the Cross-J boys had heard there was soldiers headed this way. They rode in to find out. I gather, from what Pat said, you ain't going to be no more popular than the troops would have been."

"I imagine not," Johnny agreed absent-mindedly. "Well, I reckon I'll take this baggage of mine over to the hotel and get a room, then find some chow. You haven't seen anything of Cassidy?"

"If he's in town I haven't seen him. I was

told that he lit out just as soon as the news got around that you'd killed Mitch Bailey. Bailey hung around with Cassidy and his gang, you know. Something else" — Obie paused and looked a bit troubled — "there's another rumor drifting around. Nobody's said anything to me right out yet, but some folks feel it was you killed the sheriff."

"That's crazy!"

"I know it is — but some people ain't got good sense. I'm betting some of Cassidy's crowd started the talk. It's known, of course, that Zach headed out to stop you. There's a feeling that maybe you and Zach got to shooting."

Johnny laughed shortly. "I recken folks hereabouts don't know much about the Texas Rangers."

Picking up the valise he headed down Chisholm Street in the direction of the one-story frame hotel. Here he secured a small room at the rear, then again stepped out in search of a restaurant. Seated at the counter of the first eating place he came to, he chewed meditatively and reviewed the tragic events of the day.

Finally he drained his coffee cup, paid for the meal, and again stepped outside. It was dark now. The moon wasn't yet up. A few lights shone from stores here and there along Chisholm, though it couldn't be termed a brightly lighted thoroughfare. Johnny stood on the plank walk a moment, glancing in both directions.

Half a block away a tall man was just entering a saloon. Johnny frowned suddenly. In the light from the saloon window the man's face looked familiar. "By cripes!" Johnny muttered. "That's the Ben Cassidy I knew in Santa Angela." Breaking into a quick walk, Johnny headed toward the saloon inside which the man had by now disappeared.

Johnny was just passing two darkened stores when he heard a quick soft step emerging from the shadowed passageway between them. He started to turn as a pair of muscular arms whipped about his body, pinning down his hands. Johnny twisted swiftly to one side as fresh grips took hold of him. He managed to jerk one hand free and lashed out with clenched fist. He felt his knuckles encounter someone's jaw, and a cry of pain sounded in the night. A man growled, "Shut up, dammit!"

Two more shadowy figures closed in on Johnny. He had his other hand free by this time, striking right and left. Then, as he was being borne down by the weight of superior numbers, something hard and steely crashed against the side of his head, and a thick curtain of darkness enveloped his senses.

VI. Obie Gets Tough

Deputy Obie Grant, now acting as sheriff of Painted Post, stared moodily into his glass of beer at one end of the long bar in Urban Everett's Cash Deal Saloon. Aside from its proprietor and Obie, the Cash Deal was empty. It was the oldest bar in town and didn't open as early as some of the other saloons. Urban Everett liked to sleep late and rarely opened before nine in the morning. The Cash Deal was much like other drinking places: a long bar at one side, the rest of the room occupied by a few round-topped tables and straight-backed chairs. Pictures of race horses, prize fighters, and burlesque actresses adorned the walls.

In addition to owning and operating the Cash Deal, Urban Everett was also the town mayor and justice of the peace. Doubtless had the town offered him other positions of importance he would have accepted cheerfully. He was a fat, genial man with a bald head and twinkling eyes and had earned the respect of every honest man in Painted Post. At the present moment his customary smiling countenance held an expression of puzzled exasperation.

"But I tell you, Obie," he was insisting, "a man can't just vanish into thin air. The Ranger will show up in time. Quit fretting about it."

"I don't like it," Obie said doggedly. "I should have stuck close to him until he got acquainted a mite more. Coming in here cold turkey like that, he didn't know who was his enemies and who his friends."

"You sure that's his pony at the Alamo Livery?"

"Sure!" irritatedly. "I'd know that pony in a million."

"And his things are still at the hotel?"

"Ain't I told you so?" Obie snapped. "His bed hadn't even been slept in. I traced him as far as the Texas Café, but after he ate his supper he just plumb disappeared. I checked the time with the feller that waits on the counter there. What I don't like is this: just about the time Auburn disappeared Ben Cassidy hit town."

"You blaming Ben?" Everett asked mildly.

"I don't know what to think. I just don't trust Cassidy."

"But, Obie, it's really on behalf of Cassidy and his crowd that the Ranger came here. Is it likely that Cassidy would do anything to stop the law being enforced? You got to admit that Auburn will be bucking the Cross-J. That should suit Cassidy. And, as a matter of fact," the bar proprietor added, "this disappearance should suit you, Obie. I know you ain't hankering to see the Cross-J stepped on."

"Regardless of my personal feelings," Obie growled, "the law is the law and has got to be enforced. I aim to do my best. If anything has happened to Auburn it's up to me to find out what and why. Yeah, I know — I should be glad for anything that helps Alex Jenkins, but, even so, I got to admit for the sake of honesty, if nothing else, that I sort of like Johnny Auburn. He looks like a square shooter. I was against him coming in here, in the first place, but now that he's come I got a hunch he might settle this whole business without too much trouble."

"Providing," Everett pointed out, "he hasn't left for good. Maybe the proposition was too much for him. Maybe, like some folks are hinting, he did rub out Zach Robertson — though I doubt that, myself."

"I should think you would," Obie said scornfully. "And don't get the idea, Urban, that Johnny Auburn tucked his tail between his legs and run for it. A Texas Ranger don't do such things. There ain't been much call for them to come up in this section, but down on the border they got a rep for never quitting. It would do a heap of good if folks in Painted Post got acquainted with the Rangers a mite."

"All this still doesn't explain why you think Cassidy might have made way with Auburn."

"No, it don't," Obie said promptly. "Look, Urban, I've been doing a heap of thinking. Cassidy ain't what you'd call the farmer type, yet he brings in a whole crowd to farm. It don't look natural. And some of these farmers I've talked to aren't the type hoe men would work too hard raising crops."

"Wait a minute, Obie," Everett put in. "Are you sure Cassidy brought that crowd here?"

"I sure am," Obie said flatly. "Oh, I know, Cassidy and a few friends just happened to come to Painted Post about the time the farmers arrived. Leastwise that's Cassidy's story. Even if that was true, how do you account for him getting acquainted with the farmers so soon, and visiting with them, and taking their side every time an argument comes up — just like when he talked Zach into telegraphing for soldiers to be sent here? I tell you, Cassidy is the gunman type, whether you realize it or not. He don't fit in with these farmers. His type wouldn't have the least sympathy with 'em, ordinarily."

Everett said interestedly, "All right, granted you're correct, what does it add up to?"

"Just this," Obie replied promptly. "I don't know what the game is, but I've a hunch Cassidy is up to something crooked. I can't for the life of me figure what it is; I just feel it. If that's the case, Cassidy wouldn't want a

Ranger around here. Rangers are smart, and it wouldn't be long before a Ranger would ferret out Cassidy's scheme. There's your reason for Cassidy making way with Johnny Auburn. Do I make sense?"

"You might, at that," Everett conceded. "What you aiming to do about it?"

"I'm going to drift down to the Maverick Saloon, where Cassidy hangs out when he's in town, and ask him a few questions, can I find him." And so saying, Obie gave his sombrero an angry cuff to one side and strode out of the saloon.

There were several men lined at the bar of the Maverick Saloon when Obie pushed through the swinging doors and stepped into the barroom. Three of them were Ben Cassidy, Cold-Deck Malotte, and Tascosa Jake Wiley. The others were "farmerish-looking" in their bibbed overalls and flat-heeled boots, but Obie noticed that a couple of them wore guns. They were hard-looking individuals, not at all the real farmer type. The slack-jawed Louis was at his usual place behind the bar.

Louie sided up as Obie approached the bar. "Howdy, Deputy," he greeted. "Don't often see you in here. What'll it be?"

"It won't be," Obie said shortly. "And until there's a change made I'm Sheriff Grant to you. I'm here to see Cassidy."

Cold-Deck Malotte had caught part of the conversation and turned to face Obie.

"Something wrong, Sheriff?" he asked silkily.

"There's plenty wrong," Obie growled. "I want to talk to Cassidy a mite."

Cassidy edged around to face Obie. "What's on your mind, Mister Sheriff?" he asked mockingly.

"Cassidy," Obie demanded, "where's Johnny Auburn?"

"Auburn? Johnny Auburn?" Cassidy looked surprised. "You mean that Ranger that came here last night?"

"You know damned well I do!"

Cassidy's eyes widened. "How should I know where he is? You mean he's gone?"

"Don't stall, Cassidy," Obie said angrily. "I asked a question and I want an answer."

"But, Obie, I don't know a thing —"

"I suppose you're going to tell me you didn't know he'd disappeared," Obie snapped. "It won't do any good to lie —"

Cassidy stiffened. "All right, I'll admit I've heard rumors to the effect that he'd left town," he said coldly. "Picked up that much when I was eating breakfast at the Texas Café. The feller there said you'd been asking. But I don't know anything about it. You mean you haven't found that Ranger yet? That's mighty queer."

"You're damn right it's queer," Obie said hotly. "What's queerer still is that he disappeared just about the time you hit town last night."

"Keeping cases on me, eh?"

"I sure have, but there's a lot I still aim to know. Auburn was held up on the way here by Mitch Bailey. Bailey was a friend of yours —"

Cold-Deck interposed: "Hell! Ben just had a speaking acquaintance with Bailey — like the rest of us."

"You keep out of this, Cold-Deck," Obie said grimly. "I'm talking to Cassidy. Yest'day afternoon, Cassidy, as soon as you'd heard Bailey was killed and that the sheriff had been murdered, you lit a shuck out of town as fast as your horse would carry you. Why?"

Cassidy spoke slowly, considering his words. "I don't know as I left in any particular hurry," he said steadily. "I'd been invited out to supper at Jabez Tomkins' place — that's only about eight miles out —"

"I know where it is," Obie cut in sharply.

Cassidy nodded. "In that case you know just about how long it would take me to go out there and return. There's nothing wrong with that. If your Ranger has lit out, I didn't have anything to do with it. Maybe he did kill Sheriff Robertson after all. Maybe he figured he'd better not stay here, for fear of what Robertson's friends might do."

"That last don't include you," Obie said wrathfully, "though I figure it was you who started the story that Johnny killed Zach. If I can get proof of that, Cassidy, you're going

58

to be damn sorry —"

Tascosa Jake's sneering laugh interrupted the words. "Cripes a'mighty! The new sheriff sure sounds tough. Must be all his authority has gone to his head."

Obie whirled toward Tascosa. "I'll show you just how tough I can get before this is over," he threatened.

"You ain't scaring me none, Grant," Tascosa said defiantly.

"Tascosa!" Cassidy snapped. "You hush up." Tascosa "hushed." Cassidy turned back to Obie. "I don't know just where you got the idea that I had anything to do with that Ranger's disappearance, but I'm telling you right now you're barking up the wrong tree."

"In other words," Obie accused, "you're refusing to tell what you know —"

"I don't know a damn thing —" Cassidy commenced.

"Maybe it will help your memory a mite was I to throw you in a cell and let you do some thinking." Obie was growing angrier every second, when he should have been doing some cool thinking on his own behalf.

Cassidy's eyes widened. "You'd arrest me?" Then he laughed scornfully. "You don't know what you're saying, Grant."

The laugh only served to increase Obie's wrath. "I'm arresting you," he spat. "You coming quiet?" One hand dropped to his gun butt.

"You're crazy, Grant."

"Not so crazy as you think," Obie growled. "You coming quiet or ain't you?"

"But what are you arresting me for?" Cassidy demanded.

"On suspicion of abducting, or planning the abduction of, Ranger Auburn."

"Hell! You can't hold me on any such charge. You haven't any proof. I'll just get bail and be out in no time. You're making a mistake, Grant. Your authority has gone to your head!"

"My authority," Obie said doggedly, "was passed on to me by a legally constituted member of the Texas Rangers. So long as Johnny Auburn isn't here, it's up to me to enforce the law as I see fit. Cripes! I'm sick of this palavering. Unbuckle your gun belt and hand it over."

Cassidy smiled thinly at his companions, then unbuckled his belt and gun and passed them to Obie. "There's no fool like a damned fool," he observed contemptuously. "All right, let's get going, Mister Sheriff Grant. I got ten bucks that says I'll be out of your hen-coop before one this afternoon."

"I'll take that bet," Obie snapped. "Now get going!"

Cassidy started toward the swinging doors, only pausing to say to Malotte: "You'll take care of it, Cold-Deck."

"I'll take care of it pronto, Ben," Cold-

Deck replied. "Then we'll show this tinhorn sheriff a few things about law."

Obie paused abruptly. "Mebbe you'd like to share a cell with your pal, Malotte."

Malotte hastily shook his head and turned away. Cassidy shrugged his shoulders, then, laughing softly to himself, preceded Obie through the swinging doors to the street.

Five minutes later Obie had deposited his prisoner in one of the half-dozen jail cells that were located at the rear of the sheriff's office. Entering the cell, Cassidy removed his coat and stretched comfortably out on the wooden bunk at one wall. His face still wore the same contemptuous smile.

Obie said, "I'll bring you your dinner in about an hour. Maybe you'll feel like talking then."

"You don't need to bother about dinner." Cassidy laughed coldly. "I'll be out of here by then. Just remember to bring that ten-spot. I always like to see bets paid promptly. Run along, Grant, and be sure to lock the door after you."

"You'll talk," Obie said hotly, "or you can stay here until the ants carry you out through the keyhole for all I care."

He slammed shut the door, locked it, and hastened along the corridor between cells, followed by Cassidy's mocking laughter. Once back in his office, however, he commenced to cool down and wonder if he had acted correctly. Perhaps he shouldn't have been so hasty. "No, by cripes!" he told himself stubbornly. "That Cassidy is a crook if I ever saw one. And that gang at the Maverick knows who's running the law in this town now."

Once more on the street, he headed back to the Cash Deal Saloon. There were a couple of other customers at the bar when Obie entered. Urban Everett caught his eye and motioned him down toward the far end of the bar. He said, "I hear you've arrested Cassidy, Obie. A feller just dropped in and told —"

"You're dang right I arrested the lousy crook," Obie said. "Somebody will be coming to you, I expect, in your capacity of justice of the peace to get bail for him. I'm asking you to put it high or to refuse altogether."

"I'll do what I can," Urban agreed. "What did Cassidy do to the Ranger? Where is he? You sure worked fast, Obie. Congratulations."

"I don't know what they did with Johnny, but I bet I'll find out," Obie said grimly. "Cassidy refuses to talk."

Everett's eyes widened. "You mean you arrested Cassidy without proof, Obie?"

Obie said, "I'll get proof before I'm through with that crooked son." He went on and told Everett what had happened. While he talked Everett's face grew longer and longer. Finally Obie concluded, "That's the story. I've got Cassidy where I want him now."

"Obie," Everett said seriously, "as a baby were you ever dropped hard on your head?"

"On my head . . . ?" Obie looked puzzled. "You mean — you mean I didn't do right?"

Everett said, "All you've done is wrong. You can't hold Cassidy on a charge of that kind without some proof. And I can't refuse bail."

"But — but —" Obie stammered. "I'm sure he's guilty."

"You've no proof. Not only that, but you've left yourself wide open to a charge of false imprisonment. Cassidy can sue the county. You'd better go down and let him out."

Obie's face had taken on a peculiar green color, but he was too stubborn to give up. "All right, give him bail, then, but I ain't going to withdraw the charge until I know more than I do now."

At that moment Cold-Deck came hastening into the saloon. "Everett, I want to arrange bail for Ben Cassidy."

Obie Grant didn't wait to hear the rest. He glared at Malotte and made his way out to the hitch rack in front of the saloon where he stood glumly looking down the street.

A rider from the Cross-J came loping into the hitch rack, dismounted, and tossed his reins over the crossbar. His name was Cal Henry. "Hi-yuh, Obie. What's new?" He came around the end of the hitch rack.

" 'Lo, Cal." Obie nodded shortly, then as the puncher started on toward the saloon he stopped him. "Cal, you were in town last night. Didn't see anything of Johnny Auburn around, did you?"

Cal Henry stopped. "Who? Johnny Auburn? Don't know him."

Obie explained, "That Texas Ranger that brought in the sheriff's body."

"Oh, him. No, I didn't see him. Half expected he'd be out to see Alex by this time, but he ain't showed up. What about him?"

"He's disappeared."

"T'hell you say!" The puncher stopped short. "What happened?"

Obie gave brief details. The puncher listened attentively, then said, "And you throwed Cassidy in the clink, huh? That's smart work, Obie. You must have some pretty good proof."

"I ain't telling all I know," Obie said secretively.

The puncher, seeing he could get no more news, passed on into the barroom, brushing against Cold-Deck Malotte as the man showed up carrying a paper in his hand. "All right, Sheriff." Malotte smiled thinly. "I've arranged bail. Let's go along and release Ben. He's been in that musty jailhouse too long already."

Obie gulped and said, "I'll be with you in

a minute, Malotte. I've got to see Urban first."

He pushed into the saloon, caught Everett's eye, and beckoned him toward the door. "Say, Urban, I'm caught a mite short. Could you let me have ten dollars until the first of the month?"

VII. A Wildcat for Fighting

It was the jogging of the pony that helped bring Johnny Auburn back to consciousness. First he was conscious of his aching head; then gradually it was borne in upon him that he had been thrown, like a sack of wheat, across a saddle, with his head hanging down and his hands and feet tied on either side. His head jerked with each motion of the horse, the pain helping to restore his memory. He remembered heading in the direction of the saloon where he had seen Ben Cassidy entering. Then men had attacked him from the rear. He'd put up a good fight until someone had given him that blow on the head.

His mind cleared somewhat. It was still night. Several riders surrounded him. They weren't moving fast. The horse bearing Johnny stepped into a depression on the trail and the sudden jolt brought a sharp grunt from Johnny's lips. Someone in the cavalcade of riders, hearing that grunt, called a quick order. The horses stopped. There came the creaking of saddle leather, then a man stood near Johnny's head. "You come out of it, Ranger Man?"

Johnny, his head hanging down, couldn't see the speaker. "Part way, anyhow," Johnny responded quietly.

"Look here," the man said seriously, "we don't want to make this thing any tougher than possible. You give us your word not to start another scrap and we'll tie you upright in your saddle. And add a drink of water — or whisky, as you please."

Johnny said, "I'll take the water — and give you my word."

Other men gathered close. Johnny felt his hands and feet being untied. Someone helped him to the earth. Another man held a drinking flask to his lips. The water cleared his brain. Johnny said, "What's the idea in this? Where you taking me?" It was too dark to see the faces of the men standing near, tense, as though they half expected Johnny to renew the fight.

"Boss's orders," came the reply. "You'll know more when the right time comes. Meantime, we're running this shindig. You'd better get back in that saddle now."

The surrounding men tensed, then breathed quick relief when Johnny stepped up to the saddle again. Johnny, sensing their attitude, laughed softly. "I gave my word, didn't I?" he said.

No one answered him. His hands were tied to the saddle horn in front of him. Someone else produced his sombrero and jammed it on his head. The shadowy riders closed in about him. Johnny said thanks for his hat.

The man nearest replied, "We figure to keep your gun, Ranger Man. . . . Come on, fellers, let's drift again."

The horses moved on at a faster gait now, one of them carrying double. It was too dark to make out much of his surroundings. There was a faint tinge of light along the eastern horizon, showing the moon was nearly up. Johnny judged from that he hadn't been unconscious long. Overhead the sky was sprinkled with stars. There appeared to be hills on either side. The horses were traveling at a smart gait now.

In time squares of yellow light showed ahead. Ranch buildings. The lights grew nearer. Finally the horses stopped before a long low building which Johnny judged rightly to be the bunkhouse. A door of the bunkhouse flew open, and a big man stepped out and called, "What luck?"

"We made out," replied one of the men near Johnny. "Had to use a gun barrel though."

"Cripes a'mighty!" came an angry roar. "I didn't order nothing like that."

"What you ordered, Alex, and what *we* were getting," came the dry answer, "are two different things."

The big man came hastening from the bunkhouse, swearing wrathfully. Johnny noticed that he wore whiskers and had one arm in a sling. He came up to the side of Johnny's horse, peering through the gloom. The man who had just spoken resumed, "Y'know, Alex, we didn't bargain to tame no wildcat."

Johnny said quietly, "The only Alex I know of in these parts is Alex Jenkins, owner of the Cross-J."

"You're right," the big man responded. His voice was heavy, deep, seemed to rumble from the depths of his mighty chest. "Sorry if the boys got rough with you, Auburn," he said, "but I had to see you."

Johnny said wryly, "Your ways are plumb persuasive. Do I get untied now? I'm anxious to hear your explanations."

The big man shook his head. "You won't be feeling like talking now. And we'd better keep you lashed up until I know you can listen to reason. I'll *habla* with you come morning. Good night. Take care of him, Brazos."

"We'll do that, Alex." The big man hastened off in the direction of the ranch house. Johnny was helped from his horse, but his hands weren't untied. He was taken into the bunkhouse while the others unsaddled the ponies.

"So it's the Cross-J in back of this, eh?" Johnny said, dropping into a chair with his bound hands on his lap before him.

"You guessed it." The man who had brought him inside spoke. "I'm Alex Jenkins' foreman — Brazos Burnett." Burnett was a lean, crusty-mannered man about forty years of age. He lifted his voice, "Hey, Beargrease, bring me some hot water."

A door at the far end of the bunkhouse opened, revealing what appeared to be the kitchen. A long-nosed individual with a straggly mustache stuck his head through the opening. "I got 'er on heatin', Brazos," he said. "Bring it in a few shakes of a steer's tail." Johnny judged him to be the ranch cook.

Brazos removed Johnny's hat and examined the place where the gunbarrel had landed. "Swole considerable," he grunted, "but the skin ain't broke none to speak on. I tried not to hit you too hard."

"It was you did it, eh?" Johnny said.

"Yeah, me," Burnett said calmly. "Hated to do it, but it was that, or see my hands licked. It was quicker this way." He added after a moment, "If it'll make you feel any better, you can do the same for me sometime, after we get this trouble straightened out."

"What trouble?" Johnny asked.

"Alex will tell you in the morning. I ain't talking now."

Beargrease Jones, the cook, came in with a basin of water, and Brazos commenced bathing the swollen area on Johnny's head. "You damn redhead," he muttered resentfully, half to himself, "there wa'n't no need of you making this necessary. You should have give in easy."

Johnny said quietly, "Would you have?"

Brazos growled, "Let's forget it." He continued ministering to the bruised spot.

The other punchers commenced to drift in now. They were an efficient-looking crowd, though there was little of friendliness in the looks they bent on Johnny. One man had a beautiful shiner; another had a tooth missing. Two or three others showed split cheekbones. Johnny commenced to grin. The men didn't have much to say. Johnny picked up a few of the names: Jiggs Monahan, Hub Fanning, Steve Lawson, Joe Dale, Yank Ferguson, Cal Henry, a swarthy-faced man known only as Monte. There were three or four other cowboys who hadn't been on the kidnaping expedition to Painted Post. These spent considerable time and verbiage joshing their companions about certain black eyes and cut lips.

The men were turning in now. A bunk was prepared for Johnny, though his hands were retied after he had been allowed to exercise his wrists a little and walk about a few minutes, closely guarded by two of the punchers with guns.

Brazos Burnett stood looking down at Johnny stretched out on blankets. "Don't get any idea of escaping from them rawhides, Ranger Man. We figure to leave a lamp burning on the table there, and two of the boys will be sitting on guard. One might get drowsy, but I figure they won't doze off at the same time. So you'd better forget any ideas you have of escaping, and get yourself a good night's sleep. It'll be easier that way."

Johnny lay awake for a long time after a varied assortment of snores had commenced to issue from the double tier of bunks. He eyed the two punchers seated at the table, a lamp burning brightly between them. Their guns were in holsters at their sides, and a third six-shooter lay on the table near the lamp. They weren't taking any chances. Both were watchful, wide awake. Johnny tested his bonds; they didn't give a particle. Philosophically Johnny surrendered to sleep.

VIII. An Old Bull Buffalo

The sun was high when Johnny was awakened by Brazos Burnett. "If you're ready to get up, Auburn, the boss has got some breakfast waiting for you." A strong aroma of coffee drifted in from Beargrease's kitchen. Johnny's nostrils quivered. Burnett said, "No, you'll be drinking some of Pat's coffee up to the house. Some of my crew has already et and left. You sure slept like a rock. I reckon that wallop on the head had something to do with it. How's it feel this morning?"

"I can't kick," Johnny conceded. He glanced around and saw the two guards at the table. They helped him from his bunk and led him outside before untying his hands. They held cocked guns on him while Johnny washed and then borrowed a comb for his hair. After that they retied his hands, and Burnett led the way up to the ranch house, leaving the two guards to sit down at their own breakfast. Reviewing events later on, Johnny couldn't see where he'd had one chance to make an escape. This Cross-J outfit was smart.

Mostly, though, as Johnny followed Brazos

up to the ranch house, he was thinking what Burnett had said about having "some of Pat's coffee." That would be Patricia Jenkins; Johnny wondered if she, too, approved of his abduction.

Burnett led the way through the kitchen, which was empty at present, and into the dining room of the ranch house, beyond which, through a wide archway, Johnny could see a long main room, the floor of which was covered with animal skins and Indian rugs. Sunlight poured through the windows of the dining room. At a table spread for four sat Alex Jenkins and his daughter Patricia.

Jenkins was big, with a barrellike torso and eyes like chilled steel which held youthful lights not usually seen in a man of his age. A bristly beard of iron gray hung down his chest, and his head was covered with shaggy hair of the same tone. What could be seen of the man's face, above the beard, was tanned a deep bronze. One arm was bandaged, held in a sling. His deep voice rumbled a cordial "Good morning" as Johnny was escorted by Brazos into the room. Johnny nodded coolly, without speaking, his gaze intent on the girl who had suddenly come to her feet.

Patricia Jenkins' eyes were hot, angry. Now as they fell on the rawhide thongs binding Johnny's wrists a deep flush spread over her features. Snatching a knife from the table, she started swiftly toward Johnny.

"Pat!" Alex Jenkins roared. "What you aiming to do?"

"I see no necessity for keeping him tied like an animal, Dad," the girl said indignantly.

Brazos smiled wryly. "You didn't see him in action last night."

"Hold your horses," old Jenkins growled. "I'm fixing to see 'bout that." The girl hesitated. Jenkins eyed Johnny. "We don't want to have to feed you, son," he said heavily. "You just pass your word not to cut up any monkeyshines and we'll untie them rawhide knots. I don't aim to make this any harder than necessary."

Johnny grinned suddenly. "That java smells powerful good, Mr. Jenkins. Somehow I can't help but feel I'm not going to feel very mad at anybody until I've eaten."

"Thought you'd see reason." The heavy words welled up from Jenkins' chest. "And after you've eaten you're not due to feel proddy neither. I know how Pat cooks, and she done herself proud this morning. But" — and his voice grew more serious — "just in case you do get ideas, I'm reminding you that your gun's in the bunkhouse, and Brazos and I are wearing ours. Untie those knots, Brazos."

Pat sat down while Brazos was releasing Johnny's hands, then he and Brazos took seats. Johnny sat across from the girl. At his right, at the end of the table, sat Jenkins; at the opposite end was Brazos Burnett. Both men were far enough from Johnny to prevent him from reaching either, in case he decided to make a break for freedom. The food was good. There was fried "white bacon," pancakes served with molasses, or "lick," as it was called, and golden-brown coffee. They all ate in silence, the girl rising now and then to go to the kitchen and replenish platters. Once or twice Johnny met her eyes, but she hastily looked in another direction. Breakfast was finally concluded. Patricia placed a box of cigars and Durham and papers on the table before the men. They lighted up; smoke drifted lazily in the sunlight streaming through the windows. Fresh coffee was poured around for those who wanted it.

Alex Jenkins cleared his throat. "I suppose, Auburn," he commenced, "you're wondering why we grabbed you and brought you here."

"I'm pretty good at guessing," Johnny replied quietly. "You're breaking the law here. You knew I was sent here to enforce the law. This is your way of preventing me from doing my duty. It's part of my duty to tell you, now, that you're only making more trouble for yourself. You can't buck the Rangers. You should know that."

Alex Jenkins' eyes were hard. "I deny that I'm breaking the law," he thundered. "Certain scuts come in here and started fencing off my property. I'm cutting their fences."

"The scuts, as you call them," Johnny pointed out, "have leased the land from the state. Therefore, it's not your land. Can you show me a deed to your land?"

"Deeds be blasted!" Jenkins exploded. "This was open range when I came here years and years ago. Nobody else wanted it. Ann and me — Ann was Pat's mother — figured this was our spot. I hired men, cleared certain places. This house I built with my own hands, adding to it from year to year. There's mighty few rocks in this building that I didn't lay with my own two hands. It wasn't easy. We had to fight off more than one Indian attack. But gradually we forged ahead. I've bred my stock here, year after year, rounded up and branded, rounded up and drove to market — Hell's bells! Right now I should have a herd headed for Dodge City. But with these danged nesters we haven't dared to leave. I claim the right of settlement entitled me to this land. Am I to get out now and let a lot of fool hoe men gain the product of my toil? Who settled this country, anyway? The cowmen, of course. But it's the same old story. The cowmen come in and clean up a place. Once it's peaceful, the sheepmen and the nesters follow. They ain't the guts, either of 'em, to set out and pacify their own sections. They let somebody else do the work and run the risks —"

"Wait a minute, Mr. Jenkins," Johnny said

quietly. "Even before the cowmen, didn't the buffalo hunters and the mountain men do a heap of cleaning up?"

Jenkins' fist struck the table with a crash that made the cups jump. "Yes, by Jehovah!" he thundered. "But not before all the cowmen. I've trapped and killed Injuns in the mountains. I've trailed from the Rockies to Santa Fe. I've led wagon trains and I've killed buffalo. I choose now to run cows and I've been running cows here in Painted Post Valley almost more years than you been alive. Who settled this state — the cowmen or the Texas Rangers? Cripes a'mighty! You Rangers are a mite —"

"Just a minute, Mr. Jenkins," Johnny interrupted. "I want to point out that the Rangers have been enforcing laws quite a spell. If I'm not mistaken, Stephen Austin started the Rangers back in 1823 to protect the frontier colonies from raiding tribes of Indians. You're not going to tell me" — and Johnny grinned widely — "that you were here before Austin fought the Indians."

A chuckle of amusement broke from Brazos Burnett. Johnny looked at the girl, but her face was serious. He glanced toward the end of the table where Alex Jenkins, like an old buffalo bull at bay, with his shaggy gray head and bristling whiskers, eyed him stubbornly and defiantly. A sudden angry snort left Jenkins' lips, and that deep-rumbling

78

voice worked its way through his iron-gray whiskers. "I'm not maintaining anything of the sort," he growled, "and you damn well know it. I'm just stating that no one else has the same right here as me —"

"The state of Texas —" Johnny commenced.

"Where would the state of Texas be today," Jenkins demanded, "if it had had to depend for settlement on the nesters and sheepmen? Did they come in and fight the Injuns? Did they serve through the war, when we broke from the North? Where were the nesters when the carpet-baggers come down in Texas and tried to ruin the state? You mark my word, son, it was the cowmen that saved Texas in those days, and you can talk until you're black in the face and you can't convince me you're right when you say I'm breaking the law by cutting the fences of a bunch of stinking nesters. I didn't mind when a few come in and took up land. Live and let live, says I. I even told 'em it was all right to butcher a steer for food when they needed it, though I warned 'em I'd blast merry hell out of ary man that killed a beef critter for its hide. But a few of 'em in here wasn't bad. It was when they started coming here in droves that I riz up on my hind legs and started driving 'em out."

"So far as I know to the contrary," Johnny said quietly, "they're peaceful farmers who

79

came here with certain legal rights —"

"What do you know about 'em?" Jenkins thundered. "Have you met any of 'em, talked to 'em, seen what they look like?"

Johnny smiled thinly. "I was prevented from that almost as soon as I got here. I don't think that was a wise move, either. You may get rid of one Ranger, but there are more of us to carry on if anything happens to me."

Jenkins' voice changed. "I'm sorry, Ranger Man, I had to have you brought here like this. Don't blame my men. They simply followed my orders. I'm the one responsible. But it had to be. I couldn't afford to have the law messing into my plans. We don't aim to harm you none. We're just rendering you helpless until my plans are carried out."

"The same being . . . ?" Johnny asked.

"I'm going to run every one of those damn hoe men out of here. Once they're gone I'll face the music."

"And you'll face arrest," Johnny pointed out.

"I'll chance that. There ain't much the law could do to me that would be as bad as being run off my place. I've told you why I consider this my land. Can you deny the truth of what I've said? After my plans are carried out you'll be released; then you can take such action as you see fit."

"But, Mr. Jenkins," Johnny protested,

80

"these damn hoe men, as you call them, have a right to be here. They want to raise up their families and —"

"Families!" A skeptical snort broke from Jenkins. "If you could see the kind of women they brought with 'em — those that brought any —"

"Dad!" Patricia said sharply.

A slow flush traveled up Jenkins' forehead. "I've said my say, Ranger Man," he growled. "Now you tell me where I'm wrong."

"Your big mistake," Johnny said, "was in not getting clear title to your place. I agree that you have prior, though not legal, right to the property, up to a certain point. That's what makes it hard for me. My sympathies are on your side, but the law's the law, and I'm sworn to enforce it. You're going to have to stop cutting fences. A law has been passed making fence-cutting a felony. Now, is this matter going to be settled peacefully, or do you insist on being stubborn?"

"I'm not quitting! I'm not changing my plans any!" Jenkins thundered.

"You'd better reconsider," Johnny warned. "You can't buck this whole state. I'll give you twenty-four hours to think it over. Then I'll have to act."

"And how can you act when you're a prisoner here?" Jenkins asked scornfully.

"That," Johnny replied quietly, "is something to be seen." He added, "It's up to you, Mr. Jenkins."

"I hear you." Jenkins nodded his shaggy gray head. "That works both ways. I'll give you twenty-four hours to see if you don't change your mind. On top of that, you give me your word not to step out of the ranch yard and I'll give orders you're not to be tied up again. Is it a go?"

"You're willing to trust to my word for twenty-four hours?"

"Don't know as I ever lost anything yet by trusting a man," Jenkins grunted heavily. "I reckon you Rangers are men — even if you and I don't agree on a couple of minor points."

Johnny said, "Thanks. You have my word."

IX. Orders for a Rub-out

After being released from jail by the deeply chagrined Obie Grant, Ben Cassidy, accompanied by the grinning Cold-Deck Malotte, had returned to the Maverick Saloon for a few drinks. Leaving the Maverick, Cassidy had dropped into the Texas Café for dinner, then headed in the direction of Eli Smith's General Store.

Smith himself, an elderly man with spectacles, was behind one of the long counters when Cassidy entered. Across the room was a similar counter, and behind each were tiered shelves holding various articles of merchandise. Boxes and barrels stood about on the floor. Smith's General Store was the sort of place where a man could buy anything from a forty-five cartridge to a plow, from a "sody" cracker to a sack of potatoes, from a spool of thread to a complete suit of clothing.

"Howdy, Ben," Smith greeted. "What can I do for you?"

Cassidy asked, "Did you get in any good ca'tridges yet?"

"You mean for your Colts?"

"I don't mean anything else."

"Why, it can't be more'n four-five days since you bought them N.E.P. ca'tridges, Ben —"

"You still claim they're ca'tridges, et?"

"What's wrong with 'em?" Smith frowned.

"What ain't? It'll be a couple of centuries before I buy any more. I don't like the way they foul up a barrel. I've had a couple of 'em miss fire altogether. The charge don't seem standard nohow. 'Nother thing, the shell sizes ain't all the same. Some of 'em slide sloppy-like into my cylinder; others I can't hardly push in."

Smith's frown deepened. He took down from a back shelf a partially filled box of cartridges and lifted the cover. On the sides of the box were printed the words, "National Explosive Powder Company," the capital letters of the first three words being printed in a bold red, throwing the *N, E,* and *P* into relief; the address of the company, in an Eastern state, together with other details, were printed in smaller letters below.

Smith examined the cartridges left in the box. "Well, I dunno," he said slowly. "These look all right to me, but if they don't suit you, they don't. They was well recommended —"

"By who?"

Smith flushed. "By the drummer that got me to take 'em on."

"I thought so." Cassidy chuckled. "Well, no more for me. If you got any reg'lar Colt loads in I'll take some."

"Sure, I can sell you all you want now."

Cassidy got his cartridges. He also bought a cheap green silk neckerchief, a handful of cigars, and a brassy-looking ring set with an imitation diamond.

Smith said, "Spending right free today, seems like."

Cassidy grinned. "This isn't costing me anything. I just won a bet from your dumb sheriff."

Leaving the general store with a cigar sticking at a forty-five-degree angle from his grinning lips, Cassidy strolled north on Chisholm Street until he came abreast of the sheriff's office. Here he paused to gloat at the disconsolate Obie Grant, who was seated on the small porch fronting the office. Obie looked up, scowled. He didn't say anything.

Cassidy's grin widened. "Thought maybe you'd like to know where that ten bucks went, Sheriff."

"Go away from me," Obie growled. "You smell up the atmosphere."

"How'd you like to have this?" Cassidy wiggled one finger to make his new ring sparkle. "Or this?" — fingering the bright green neckerchief. His sneering laugh grated on Obie's nerves.

Obie said insultingly, "That ring will be as

85

green as your bandanna come a month or so. What kind of a stone is that — a chunk of beer bottle?"

Cassidy chuckled good-naturedly. "Whatever it is, money bought it, Sheriff. Ain't you pleased?" Obie didn't say anything. Eying him contemptuously, Cassidy leaned back against the hitch rack and commenced plucking cartridges out of his cartridge belt. One by one he sneeringly flipped the loads on the porch at the sheriff's feet.

Obie looked surprised. "Have you gone cuckoo?"

"Yeah — like a fox." Cassidy grinned widely. "I'll donate these to your office. Lord knows this county is going to be glad of a few donations before I get through with it."

"What do you mean by that?" Obie asked suspiciously.

Cassidy didn't reply at once. He drew out his six-shooter, watched narrowly by the sheriff, plucked out the cartridges and tossed them on the porch, then reloaded with his newly purchased loads which he took from a trousers' pocket. When he had also replenished the empty loops in his belt he explained in a tantalizing drawl. "Well, if you must know, Obie, my boy," he said, "I'm laying plans to sue this county for false arrest and imprisonment. By the time I get through with you, you'll wish you'd never heard of Ben Cassidy. It will mean your job, of course, but that ain't worrying me none."

Obie squirmed. "All right, I made a mistake," he conceded.

"A mistake, he calls it!" Cassidy laughed uproariously. "By God, before I get through with this county the authorities will think you've set off a calamity. I've got this county just where I want it. From now on I call the tune and you'll dance. I'll make you wish —"

"Cut it short!" Obie rose to his feet, anger getting the better of him. Somewhat taken aback, Cassidy paused, his eyes widening at the wrath in Obie's face. Obie went on, "Cassidy, you can sue and be damned! Sure, I'll lose my job, but remember — I'm still sheriff in Painted Post. And until I lose my job you'd better tread mighty careful. I won't make a second mistake. I'm not sure, even now, that you're not guilty of something that's damned fishy around here. When I get proof, look out — whether I've lost my job by that time or not — because, Cassidy, I'll get you and I'll get you right. Now get to hell out of here. Every time I breathe I get to thinking a skunk has whelped on my doorstep. Go on, git!"

Cassidy opened his mouth to speak, closed it, then, overcome by the righteous anger blazing in Obie's eyes, he remained silently leaning against the tie rail until the sheriff had finished. Finally he said somewhat defiantly, "No use you taking this to heart, Obie.

After all, I got my rights —"

"I ain't sure you have," Obie snapped. "I've told you once to git. Cassidy, you'd better git!"

Forcing a laugh, Cassidy turned and strolled off in the direction of the Maverick Saloon.

Obie sank back in his chair and mopped perspiration from his forehead. "Dammit!" he muttered. "There I've lost my temper again. Now Cassidy will start suit against the county and I'll find myself up Hard-Luck Creek. I wish I could learn to keep my big mouth shut — or maybe I don't. I dunno what to think." He slumped disconsolately back in his chair, then, his gaze falling on the cartridges scattered at his feet, he rose, stooped down and retrieved them, one by one, and settled back again, mumbling angrily to himself.

His forehead wrinkled as he looked at the loads. "N.E.P. ca'tridges, eh? Can't say I blame Cassidy for throwing such junk away, but he sure riled me, stuffing those fresh loads in his gun — me knowing I'd paid for 'em." He rose disgruntledly and retired to his office, carrying the discarded cartridges with him.

Cassidy, meanwhile, had entered the Maverick and found Malotte and Tascosa Jake drinking at a table. A few customers were being served by Louie at the bar. Cassidy dropped into a chair between his two henchmen and refused the drink Malotte offered. He displayed his new ring and neckerchief, then passed out cigars. "On the sheriff" — he grinned — "but he didn't send on his compliments with 'em. Grant is sore as a boiled owl. He like to jump right down my throat a spell back; he was that mad."

Malotte chuckled. "You sure got him in a pickle. Me and Tascosa were just wondering when you'd start suit against the county. You got a clear case, Ben, every way we look at it."

Cassidy considered. Finally, "One thing at a time, Cold-Deck. Right now I'm not starting any suit, though I figure to keep the sheriff worried about it. I'd like to finish our present game first. The suit can wait. A suit might drag on for some time. There might be investigations made. Until a suit was decided in my favor Grant might retain his sheriff's office. He might get a chance to make it tough for us. Hell! I can sue the county any time within the next year or so."

Malotte could see the sense of the decision and nodded agreement.

Tascosa said, "But what in hell did become of that Ranger?"

"I've been thinking over that too," Cassidy replied. "We know we had nothing to do with it. It's a cinch the sheriff didn't, even if Grant, maybe, wouldn't want Auburn coming into his jurisdiction. Who else would want Auburn out of the way?"

Malotte and Tascosa Jake considered, finally gave it up.

"Hell!" Cassidy said impatiently. "Use your brains. It can't be anybody else but Alex Jenkins."

"Alex Jenkins!" Malotte repeated unbelievingly.

"Certain," from Cassidy. "He doesn't want any Ranger checking into this game any more than we do — not as much, in fact. *We* might get a break from Auburn, but not Jenkins. Jenkins is breaking the law to all intents and purposes."

"I'll be damned!" Tascosa swore. "I believe you're right, Ben. It must be Jenkins. I wonder if he had the Ranger dry-gulched."

"I don't think so," Cassidy said slowly. "Jenkins hasn't sense enough for that. He's one of these damned fools that has moral scruples against killing."

"Where do you figure Auburn is, then?" Malotte wanted to know.

Cassidy yawned. "If I ain't bad mistaken," he said, "Ranger Auburn is being held a prisoner out to the Cross-J."

"Hell's bells!" Tascosa protested. "They can't hold him prisoner indefinitely."

"They probably could," Cassidy contradicted, "but I don't figure they intend to. They'll just hold him long enough."

"Long enough for what?" Cold-Deck asked.

"That's what I'd like to know," Cassidy replied. "But you can bet your life that Jenkins has some scheme up his sleeve. He won't give up easy. You both know what a hellion he is — a regular range bull on a rampage when he gets mad. No, I don't like it at all."

"All right," Malotte put in, "granting that Auburn is held prisoner out to the Cross-J, what are we going to do about it? You aiming to set him free, Ben? If so, it'll be tough, bucking Jenkins' crew. That's one salty crew and don't forget it."

"Maybe I got a better idea," Cassidy said. His hearers waited. Cassidy went on, "Supposing Auburn was found dead out there on the Cross-J?"

"By God, that's an idea!" Tascosa exclaimed. "If it could be made to look like Jenkins had had him murdered — Geez! Ben, you got a head on you. It would all look natural enough. Everybody would realize Jenkins didn't want a Ranger interfering. Cripes a'mighty! It's a cinch. We'll have that ol' buffalo bull right by the short hair. Once get him outten our way and we'll have clear sailing —"

"Admitted," Malotte put in, "but who is going to kill Auburn?"

"I've thought of that too." Cassidy smiled coolly. "Tascosa, it looks like a job for you."

"I'll take on the job of rubbing out a

Ranger any time, and glad of it," Tascosa said boastfully. "When do I start?"

"In a little while," Cassidy replied. "Here's what I want you to do. Take one man with you —"

"Hell! I can do it alone," Tascosa commenced.

"Shut your mouth until I finish," Cassidy snapped. "I said to take one man with you. I'm giving orders for this rub-out. I'm not going to take a chance on one man missing it, if he gets a shot at Auburn. The two men drawing a bead is safer. Is Pearly Gates around town?"

Malotte glanced toward the bar. "He was in having a drink not twenty minutes ago. I reckon he's around town someplace."

Cassidy nodded and turned back to Tascosa. "I want Pearly to go with you. He'll be under your orders. Pearly ain't overly burdened with brains, but he can sure shoot like hell. You two wait until the sun gets lower, then slope out to the Cross-J. Keep out of sight. Spy out the ground. If Auburn is there — and I feel sure he is — keep him under observation. When the time is right, get as close as you can without being discovered, draw your beads, and let him have it."

"The plan sounds good to me," Tascosa said eagerly. "I just want to get that Ranger in my sights once and —"

"Do your talking afterward," Cassidy cut in

coldly. "Wait until you've downed Auburn before you start running off at the head. This job won't be easy. Once it's done you'll have to get away fast —"

"We'll head our ponies north, then swing wide," Tascosa interrupted again. "That'll throw trailers off the track."

"You'll do nothing of the sort," Cassidy snapped. "You'll head back for town as fast as your broncs will carry you. What's the sense of traveling all over the country when you can lose your tracks right down Chisholm Street as soon as you arrive? Tracks in open country are easy to read, but I never yet saw a trailer good enough to pick sign out of a well-traveled road that's churned up by a lot of riders. Now go find Pearly and tell him what's up. Tell him I'm paying well for the job. Get a move on."

Tascosa rose. "Right," he said eagerly, one hand already fingering his gun butt. "This is a job to my liking. Don't fear, Ben. That Ranger is as good as stony cold already."

X. Shots in the Night!

The rest of the day, after breakfast, passed pleasantly enough for Johnny Auburn. He wandered about the ranch buildings, talking to two or three of the hands who were working at home that day. In the cookhouse he gave Beargrease Jones a new recipe for flapjacks; he helped Hub Fanning bend new tires on one of the chuck wagons that stood in need of repair. Before the day was half over the Cross-J hands had just about decided that Johnny Auburn was an "all-right hombre," though the circumstances of the situation demanded they maintain a not-too-friendly attitude, considering that, from the viewpoint of the man who paid their wages, the Ranger was an enemy.

It was while Johnny was helping Hub Fanning with the chuck wagon that Cal Henry returned with the mail from Painted Post. Cal was a lean, blond young fellow with sleepy eyes and a sense of humor. After leaving the mail sack at the ranch house he paused on his way to the corral to sit his saddle, smiling lazily at Johnny and Fanning.

Fanning wiped sweat from his brow and

looked up. Johnny also straightened his lean form and surveyed the rider. Fanning grunted, "You, Cal, what's striking you so funny? If your back was nigh broke from bending over this wheel —"

"Don't let me interrupt," Cal said politely. "I just thought maybe you'd like to hear the news from town." He looked at Johnny. "In a way it concerns you."

Johnny said, "Yeah? Spill it."

"Just as I was dropping into the Cash Deal for a swallow of dust chaser," Cal went on, "I run into Obie Grant. Obie wa'n't looking too cheerful. Right away he asks me if I'd seen Ranger Auburn when I was in town last night. Course I said no."

Johnny smiled faintly. "Thereby proving yourself a liar. If I'm not mistaken, it was my fist that made that cut on your lip last night."

Cal Henry nodded. "Now that you mention it, maybe I am a liar — but it's all in a good cause." He ran one hand meditatively over a slight abrasion on his lower lip. "Maybe I'm lucky, too," he conceded, "that I didn't have to tackle you alone. I hope there ain't any hard feelings, Ranger Man."

"None that can't be squared sometime later," Johnny said quietly.

Cal looked uncomfortable. "I ain't sure I like the way you said that," he said wryly. "I'd better get back to my news. It's all over town, and a heap of hombres are having a good laugh at Obie Grant's expense."

"How come?" Johnny wanted to know.

"It's like this," Cal explained. "When you disappeared Obie took it for granted that Ben Cassidy was back of your abduction. From all I hear" — dryly — "Ben didn't have a thing to do with it. Howsomever and whatever, Obie didn't wait for proof. He was so set in his own mind that Cassidy had been up to the aforesaid skulduggery, that he quick as a wink slammed Cassidy in the jug and charged him with most dire proceedings."

An abrupt howl of laughter left Hub Fanning's lips. "Oh, cripes a'mighty!" he gurgled. "That's good! Cassidy thrown in the hoosegow for what we done. That's the best ever!" He went off into another paroxysm of glee, bent nearly double over the wagon wheel upon which he'd been working.

Johnny grinned. "Good for Obie. I've got one friend in these parts anyway. He may have been mistaken, but Cassidy needed jailing, I'm betting."

"I admire your sentiments," Cal continued, "appreciating, as I do, the thought behind your words, but I begs to point out that it ain't good for Obie a-tall. As a matter of fact, affairs for the minion of the law shape up very darkly indeed. In short, Sheriff Obie Grant has got himself into one hell of a jam, and he ain't seeing no method to lift him out of said precarious position. Do I make myself clear?"

"You do not," Johnny said. Hub was still chuckling, waiting to hear more. Johnny added, "Elucidate a mite."

"Elucidate — a very good word," Cal said appreciatively. "I'll use it at the first opportunity. But, to continue with my tale: when Obie arrested Cassidy, Cassidy offered to bet ten bucks that he'd be out on bail very shortly. Showing an entire lack of foresight, Obie took the bet. Obie is now ten dollars short. What is more, the aforesaid Benjamin Cassidy, Esquire, is threatening to sue the county for false arrest, false imprisonment, and defamation of character."

"Which last would be quite a job, if I know Cassidy," Johnny put in.

"I'm surmising in the same direction." Cal nodded. "Probably by the time some shyster lawyer gets the case it will also be claimed that Obie caused Ben Cassidy extreme mental anguish, or something of the sort. Anyway, Obie is squirming like a hawg in a barrel of boiling oil — and there don't seem no surcease in sight. To add to his misery, folks are insisting the drinks are on him. Obie don't deny the allegation, but, being as the payment of his bet left him broke, he finds himself unable to comply — which same only heightens his misery."

Johnny produced some bills from his pocket and peeled off a ten-spot. "If you go in tomorrow," he said, "I'd appreciate your leaving this in Obie's desk sometime when he isn't around. I owe him that much, I figure."

"I already left a ten-spot when he wasn't in — on my way out of town. Obie's a friend, and I didn't think he should have to pay for his friendship. I'll take one buck, though, and get more from the other boys. Hub, you can kick a buck into the collection. You already had a dollar's worth of amusement."

Cal furnished further details, then continued on his way to the corral. Johnny and Hub finished their work on the wagon wheel. When it was done Hub said "Much obliged" in a grateful voice, and Johnny strolled off in search of something else to fill his time.

On the long front gallery of the ranch house he found Patricia Jenkins looking over some mail. She saw him passing and hailed him. "Here's a couple of newspapers from Fort Worth, if you're interested."

"I reckon I am." He smiled and stepped up on the long flagstone porch. Finding a chair not far from the girl, he opened a newspaper, though he couldn't greatly interest himself in its contents. After a time he looked up and found Pat Jenkins gazing at him.

The girl said directly, "I reckon you're hating us, aren't you, keeping you prisoner this way?"

"I didn't say that," Johnny replied quietly. "It could be much worse. You could have kept me trussed up like a thrown calf all this time. Instead, you've allowed me my freedom, within certain limits. I'd be a fool not to appreciate that. I don't like it, naturally."

The girl said a trifle bitterly, "Do you think *we* like it? After all, we didn't ask you to come here."

"You certainly didn't," Johnny said dryly. "Your hands just grabbed me and brought me here, whether I liked it or not."

"I mean we didn't ask you to come to Painted Post."

"Governor Ireland did. That is, he asked that a Ranger be sent here. There's a job to do, Miss Jenkins. If I don't do it, some other Ranger will. Your father should recognize that fact. He can't lick the Rangers. Sooner or later he'll realize that he's up against something tougher than he is."

Pat Jenkins didn't reply at once. She sat moodily staring off down the valley. Hills rose on either side, dotted with cedar and post oak. Overhead a few fleecy clouds floated serenely against the turquoise sky. She said rather abruptly, "You think Father is making a terrible blunder of this, don't you?"

Johnny said quietly, "What do you think?"

"It's not my place to think," she responded readily. "Dad has always done the thinking for the Cross-J. So far he hasn't made a bad job of it. The men obey him blindly." She shrugged her shoulders slightly. "What's good enough for the men is good enough for me. I've seen Father in action before. Oh yes, there have been other troubles. Show me a cowman who doesn't have troubles — drought, rustlers, disease. Dad has always won in the end, regardless of odds."

"This," Johnny said, "is different. I think even you are wondering this time if he is right."

The girl looked at him. Johnny met her gaze steadily. After a moment she glanced off along the valley again. "It's not my place to even wonder," she said slowly. "I'll trail with Dad. Look at it any way you like, Johnny Auburn, we're enemies."

"Do we have to be?"

"I don't see how it can be otherwise. Ben Cassidy and his gang are set to rob Dad of the Cross-J. You're sent here to block Dad's moves. I'm loyal to Dad, naturally."

Johnny said definitely, "You can't expect to set the law aside simply because your father neglected to get title to these lands. That could have been accomplished long ago with slight trouble."

Pat Jenkins' dark eyes flashed. "Can't you understand that Dad didn't realize how things would be? He's been here most of his life. He settled this country. Do you wonder he claims it? Surely the state of Texas won't begrudge him the land he's held so long — but, yes, I guess it does. But, regardless of law, Dad has a right to this valley — far more right than Ben Cassidy or any other man. Can't you see that?"

"What I see and what the law sees are two different things," Johnny pointed out. "Your father is living in the past when the six-shooter was law. The day of settling problems with gunpowder is passing fast. The instant the farmers started to come in you should have hired a good lawyer —"

"We tried that," the girl interrupted. "We consulted an attorney in Fort Worth. I guess he must have been an honest man, for he said frankly he'd rather not take the case. He pointed out that there was little use in Dad trying to get title now, when the farmers already held state leases. He was willing to go to the courts with the matter, if we insisted, but he wouldn't promise anything. I was inclined to at least let him try, but Dad lost his temper and tore out of the attorney's office, saying he'd settle things in his own way. So there you are. And Dad's gone too far to let you interfere in his plans."

Johnny rolled and lighted a cigarette. Neither spoke for several minutes. Tobacco smoke curled lazily in the air. Johnny considered the matter. Finally he asked, "How large are your holdings?"

Patricia smiled. "I don't believe even Dad knows. He's always claimed this whole valley. Roughly it takes in probably a hundred and fifty sections."

"That's close to a hundred thousand acres."

"Between ninety and a hundred thousand." The girl nodded.

Johnny considered. "There are other cattlemen in these parts. Don't they own their land either?"

"Oh yes, they all hold title, I believe. But they don't like the nesters coming in any better than Dad does. They're on his side. They're good friends of ours. There's John Barr, owner of the 33-Bar outfit; Herman Scott, who runs the Box-S; Charlie Fitzherbert, of the Circle-Slash, and three or four others on either side of our valley. They respected Dad's claims. If I'm not sadly mistaken they'll fight to back him up. So you see what you're in for, Ranger Man."

Johnny smiled. "They're beyond the Painted Post Mountains and the Little Painted Posts, I suppose."

"They could get here in a hurry." Pat's words held a certain threat that Johnny didn't miss.

His smile widened. "And a little foresight could have saved so much bloodshed and hard feelings," he told the girl. "It's not right that other men should be pulled into the

Cross-J's troubles, do you think?"

Pat looked uncomfortable. "They're Dad's friends," she said stubbornly. "He's helped them more than once."

"I believe that. And yet it's a shame to think that this land could have been had for so little money at one time. A few cents an acre would have covered the price —" He paused suddenly, then, "Maybe I'm a fool," he said, half to himself.

The girl frowned. "I don't understand."

Johnny didn't answer at once, then, "Maybe I don't, myself, yet, but I just happened to think of something."

"Something that will settle all this trouble?"

"Maybe," Johnny said reluctantly. "I'm not sure. I just had a sudden hunch. It might work out; again it might not."

"What is it?"

Johnny shook his head. "I don't want to say yet. But you can help. Get your Dad to promise not to cut any more wire, and I'll see what I can do."

The girl suddenly rose to her feet, smiling coldly. "It doesn't work, Ranger Man. We don't like tricks."

"You think I'm tricking you into something?"

"You refuse to state what you have in mind. We can't take chances. I know Dad wouldn't take chances on a thing of that kind."

Johnny smiled wryly at the girl. "Reckon I'll have to go it alone then, Miss Jenkins."

Pat didn't reply but turned and went into the house.

The subject wasn't reopened again that night at supper, which Johnny ate with Alex Jenkins, Pat, and Brazos Burnett. No one spoke to any extent. After supper, when Johnny made a move to leave for the bunkhouse, Alex Jenkins stopped him.

"I'd rather you'd stay here," Jenkins said shortly. He didn't explain why. Johnny heard several riders leave the corral and judged they were being sent with messages somewhere. He guessed something unusual was in the wind but couldn't figure what it was. Neither Brazos nor Jenkins referred to the matter. Supper over, the four went to the big main room of the ranch house. The men smoked in silence. Pat had little to say. Whether or not she had told her father of their conversation of the afternoon, he didn't know. He guessed she hadn't; but that she was still mulling over his words, he felt certain.

Jenkins belatedly brought out cigars and a bottle of bourbon, as though suddenly remembering his duties as host, but neither the drinks nor the tobacco melted the hostility that lay heavy in the air. Beyond a few words now and then, no one had a great deal to say. Shortly after ten-thirty the sounds of a couple of returning riders were heard. A little later Jenkins gave Johnny permission to go to the bunkhouse.

"I'm not forgetting," he said determinedly, "that you gave me your word not to try to escape until twenty-four hours had passed. I don't want to have to tie you up tonight."

"My word is still good," Johnny said stiffly.

Jenkins nodded shortly. Johnny said good night to Pat, who replied with a brief word or two, and preceded Brazos Burnett toward the rear of the house, followed by Alex Jenkins. The oil lamp was turned low in the kitchen. Brazos turned up the wick as they passed through. Johnny opened the kitchen door. For a moment he stood there, framed against the yellow light in the opening, breathing in the freshness of the cool night air. Across the ranch yard, a short distance, lights gleamed from the bunkhouse windows.

Johnny was about to step outside when he felt a hand on his shoulder, then heard Brazos' voice: "Just a minute, Auburn. I'll go first. I want to make sure the boys in the bunkhouse aren't talking too loud." He jerked Johnny back, adding, "There's things you shouldn't hear —"

That was all that saved Johnny. As Brazos pulled him back two leaden slugs plowed savagely into the woodwork of the doorjamb. Instantly came the heavy double report of exploding guns. A third shot whined viciously through the kitchen, coming from the thick

105

brush that surrounded the ranch yard. Instinctively Johnny's right hand dropped to the spot where his holster should have been. Then he remembered: his gun and belt hadn't been returned to him. He was unarmed!

XI. One against Many

"Hell's bells!" Alex Jenkins roared angrily. "That last shot nigh got me."

For a brief moment Brazos was too surprised to speak. While he stood there, lips trying to form the words that refused to come, Johnny whirled, his right hand stabbing at the gun in Brazos' holster. The next instant he had leaped through the doorway, the six-shooter clutched in his fist. From within the house he heard Pat's sharp cry of alarm. Behind were hoarse bellowings from Brazos and Alex Jenkins.

As he sprinted across the ranch yard toward the point where he had last seen the flash of gunfire another shot lanced from the brush surrounding the yard, then another.

But Johnny was moving too fast to make a good target. He lifted Brazos' gun. Crimson fire spurted from the muzzle. Again he fired. A sharp cry of pain rose in the night.

Johnny closed in fast. A bullet snarled past his face. He thumbed one more swift shot. As he reached the brush the sudden creaking of saddle leather, then the pounding of horse's hoofs reached his ears. He knew the rider was plunging through the brush, making for the open trail.

Johnny stopped short, ears tense to pick up the direction. He whipped up the gun. The hammer moved twice under his thumb, each time throwing sharp flashes of smoke and flame. As the hammer dropped the next time it fell on an empty shell. Johnny swore softly to himself and lowered the gun. He could still hear the hoofbeats. They were farther away now.

There were wild yells from the bunkhouse by this time. Brazos and Jenkins came plunging up, talking angrily in loud voices. Jenkins asked, "Who was it?"

Johnny said, "You got me. One of 'em got away, headed toward Painted Post. I think I nicked the other one." He turned toward Brazos, extending the gun. "Here's your hawg-laig. I could wish the cylinder had had a full load."

"Always figured five loads was safer."

"I reckon you're right," Johnny conceded. He headed toward the brush, followed by Jenkins and Brazos, the latter stuffing fresh cartridges into his gun. A couple of hands came running from the bunkhouse, carrying a lighted lantern and asking questions. They didn't have far to go into the brush. First they saw the saddled horse tethered to a low mesquite tree, then a couple of yards away was the body of a man, sprawled on his face, one lifeless hand still clutching a Winchester rifle. The lantern was moved closer. Brazos turned the body on its back. After a moment he said grimly, "That was smart shooting, Auburn."

"Lucky, more likely," Johnny said shortly. "Who is he? Anybody know him?"

One of the hands, lanky Yank Ferguson, spoke up. "Hell, yes! That there corpse is known as Pearly Gates. Had quite a rep as a sharpshooter. Mean bustard — the kind that was always pluggin' dogs just to see 'em squirm. Pro'bly humans, too, when he got the chance."

Johnny said, "This time he took one chance too many. Where's he from?"

"You got me." Yank shrugged. "He hung around Painted Post with the Cassidy gang."

Cal Henry came plunging up on a pony, followed by another rider. "Got here as fast as we could saddle up, Alex," he panted. "What way did the dirty dry-gulching son take?"

"Toward town," Alex replied, "but you might as well put them broncs back in the corral. That feller's got too much start toward Painted Post for you to overtake him. And you'd just lose his tracks in town. Let it go for tonight, you and Joe. A couple of you boys can take this body into Painted Post come morning."

"I'll take the blame for the shooting,"

Johnny put in. "Just tell Obie I did it."

"You'll do nothing of the sort, Cal," Alex said sharply. Then to Johnny, "It don't work, Auburn. Obie isn't going to learn you were here — not just yet."

Johnny laughed softly. "I didn't count much on it working."

Jenkins snorted scornfully. "We ain't fools." His voice softened a trifle. "Auburn, you had a gun in your hand. You could have got away."

Johnny said in surprised tones, "I gave my word —"

"Yeah, I know," Jenkins growled, "but a heap of men would forget a passed word, once they was loose and had a gun. You acting square like that makes it hard what I'm going to do. You can take back your word." He spoke swiftly to Brazos and leveled his own six-shooter.

Johnny frowned at the two gun barrels pointed at him. "I don't just get the idea," he said easily.

"I was afraid you wouldn't," Jenkins said uncomfortably. "I hate like sin to do this, Auburn, but I'm going to tie you up again. You've got to stay in the bunkhouse — No, wait, I know what you're about to say. It ain't that I don't trust your word, but this is for your own good. I figure those shots were meant for you. You stood in that kitchen doorway long enough to be recognized. Ben

110

Cassidy framed this deal or I'm a liar."

Brazos said surprisedly, "I don't get your idea, Alex. Auburn is supposed to be here to back Cassidy's play. Why should he want Auburn rubbed out?"

Jenkins said impatiently, "It would look damn bad for me if Auburn's body was found on the Cross-J. That would fit in fine with Cassidy's plans, I figure. I'm playing too big a game to take chances on that now. Two men tried to dry-gulch this Ranger tonight. No telling but what somebody else may try it tomorrow, if Auburn is wandering around loose. But if we keep him in the bunkhouse, under guard, nothing won't happen."

"Maybe that's smart." Brazos nodded.

"I sure hate to do it," Jenkins went on apologetically to Johnny. "This makes it seem like I broke my own word. But this is for your own good. It won't be for long. I figure we can cut you loose after tomorrow night —" He halted suddenly.

"What's tomorrow night?" Johnny asked. "More wire-cutting?"

"You guessed wrong," Jenkins said. "But it's for me to know and you to find out. All right, mosey along to the bunkhouse, Auburn. We'll try to make it as easy as possible. I hope you won't kick up any trouble."

"I reckon I won't — not right away, leastwise," Johnny admitted as he headed for the bunkhouse with the guns of Brazos and

111

Jenkins following every move. As he stepped into the bunkhouse he heard Pat calling from the house to learn what had caused the shooting. Her father replied briefly, then followed Johnny inside the building and watched closely while Johnny's hands were once more tied behind his back.

Two guards, Cal Henry and Yank Ferguson, watched over Johnny that night. Once in blankets, Johnny went promptly to sleep. During the night he heard a couple of riders arrive and shortly afterward enter the bunkhouse and get into bunks. The lamp on the bunkhouse table was kept burning throughout the night, and both Yank and Cal were alert. Stretched in his bunk, hands tied behind him, there was small opportunity for Johnny to get free. Johnny woke before daylight. The first thing that entered his mind was Alex Jenkins' statement of the night before: "We can cut you loose after tomorrow night." That meant tonight, now. What was scheduled to happen today or tonight?

Johnny watched gray light come through the windowpanes as he dwelt on the problem. Gradually the room grew brighter, making clearer the long tier of double bunks along one wall, the mess table at the far end of the bunkhouse, near the entrance to the kitchen where Beargrease Jones was already making a great to-do with pans and food and kettles. Across the room, almost opposite him, Cal and Yank had commenced to yawn at their table. The flame of the oil lamp between them was starting to pale in the growing dawn. After a time men appeared, crawling out of their bunks.

Cal and Yank said good morning when they saw Johnny's eyes were open. They released his hands and rubbed his numbed arms and wrists before taking him outside to wash up. They had little to say. Back at the breakfast table, again the same situation prevailed. The men talked but little, and a tense something seemed to hover in the atmosphere.

When the meal was finished Johnny's wrists were bound behind his back again. He was given his choice of a chair or returning to his bunk. He chose the bunk; it seemed less awkward to stretch out at full length. Besides, he could think better if the Cross-J hands thought he was asleep. Yank and Cal crawled into blankets and were soon snoring lustily. Hub Fanning took over the guard job now. Apparently, it was felt only one guard would be necessary in the daytime. The other men, one by one, passed outside. Hub wasn't talkative either. Now and then, when he saw that Johnny's eyes were open, he'd roll a cigarette and hold it between Johnny's lips while he smoked, but by this time his growing friendliness of the previous day had entirely disappeared.

What was it that was due to happen tonight? Johnny considered the problem from all directions and couldn't arrive at any definite conclusion. Then suddenly Johnny discovered something else: the length of pine board at the back of his bunk had once held a half section of knot imbedded in the top of the wood. Later the knot had fallen out, leaving a depression the shape of a half circle. And one side of that half circle provided a rather sharp edge. Just how long that resin-impregnated sharpness would last, Johnny wasn't certain, but by twisting to lie on his right side he found he could manipulate the rawhide thongs binding his wrists against that edge. It might be possible, in time, to cut through the rawhide.

Anyway, it was worth trying, and it helped Johnny pass the time. It was necessary, of course, to keep a sharp eye that Hub wasn't watching him, and he had to work carefully so as not to be discovered. When dinnertime came he refused to eat, saying he had a headache. The men sympathized with him but, suspecting some trick, made no offer to release him. Johnny, of course, didn't want anyone touching those rawhide thongs now. The afternoon drifted past quite swiftly. Johnny couldn't tell how much progress he was making against that knot edge, but he thought his bonds did feel just a trifle looser. He admitted, however, it may have been his imagination playing tricks. Anyway, he continued working stealthily on the rawhide whenever he could do so unobserved by his guard. When supper came he again refused to eat. The crew seemed to think little of his attitude, occupied as it was with problems of its own.

From his bunk Johnny watched the men at the long supper table. They ate in silence. A certain tenseness showed in every face. Even Cal Henry, usually the most talkative, had little to say. Brazos Burnett came in right after supper. "All right, boys," he ordered. "You'd better get saddled up."

In the light from the oil lamps his face looked worn and lined. He paused a moment beside Johnny's bunk. "I'm sorry about this, Auburn, but we'll let you go first thing in the morning." Without awaiting an answer he turned and hurried from the bunkhouse.

What was being planned for tonight? Johnny worked a little harder at his bonds. "Cripes," he told himself, "I've simply got to get out of this. There's something big afoot and I'm not even invited."

One by one the men took their guns and left the bunkhouse, until only Hub Fanning was left on guard with Johnny. In the kitchen Beargrease Jones was making a great clatter with pans and dishes as he washed up the supper mess. Finally he, too, blew out his lamp and came in, taking off the sugar sack he wore for an apron. Johnny watched while Beargrease loaded two shotguns, then studied them, as though uncertain which to take with him. Eventually he stood one in a corner, strapped on a six-shooter, and hurried from the building.

By this time there was a great deal of noise floating in from the night air. Saddle leather creaked; horses stomped, then moved off in, Johnny judged, the direction of the ranch house. There was considerable talk from outside, too, though Johnny couldn't distinguish the words. He looked at Hub, who appeared to be uneasy.

"Weren't you invited to the party, Hub?" Johnny asked.

"I'm invited, all right," Hub said, even-voiced. "All hell couldn't keep me away. I'll be leaving right quick now, so if there's anything you want — cigarette or drink of water — you'd better say so."

Johnny shook his head. "You don't mean you're going to leave me here all alone?"

"You won't be able to go anyplace," Hub grunted. "When we get back we'll cut you loose — then you can go on with your damn law-enforcing."

"Where you heading, anyway, Hub?" Johnny asked.

"You'll find out, come morning," Hub said shortly.

A step sounded at the door. Cal Henry entered. "All right, Hub. I got your bronc saddled. Alex says to come on. Even if Auburn does manage to wiggle loose after we've gone it'll be too late for him to do anything about it." He spoke to Johnny: "Sorry you can't honor us with your presence, Ranger Man. There's something big cooking up —"

"Cut the palaver," Hub said roughly, already headed toward the doorway. "Come on now, Cal — you're wasting time."

Cal said *"Adiós"* in a mocking voice and hurried after his partner. Johnny was left alone in the bunkhouse.

For a brief moment he lay in his bunk, eying the single oil lamp burning on the table. If he just could get to that table, knock over the lamp, start a fire . . . That would bring back the men in a hurry. Or would it? Already the sounds of Hub's and Cal's departure had passed from hearing. A turmoil of emotions broke loose in Johnny. He struggled frantically against the rawhide thongs and only succeeded in scraping raw the skin on his wrists. He worked the rawhide furiously against that sharp edge where the pine knot had been, but the edge appeared to be dulled by this time.

Johnny gave up that idea. It would have to be the lamp. He'd have to run the risk of being burned alive before help could arrive. Twisting to one side, he threw his feet from the bunk and stood up. He reached the table

117

in two long strides, then paused. There was a step at the door, and Pat Jenkins rushed in.

The girl's face was ashen. "Johnny!" she cried. "You've got to stop them. You were right! We can't buck the law. It will just mean more bloodshed. Oh, stop them before they leave!"

"Steady, Pat." Johnny spoke rapidly. "Get me untied. Wait, there's a knife on the table. Hurry!"

The girl sawed at his bonds. Johnny thought they'd never be cut through. Apparently he hadn't made much headway against that knot edge. Finally the rawhides parted. Johnny's hands were free. He turned to the girl again, rubbing life back into his numbed fingers. He asked questions. The girl's words wouldn't come at first. Time was slipping fast. Johnny placed both hands on the girl's shoulders. "Steady," he said again. "Tell me what's afoot. Talk fast — there isn't much time."

His words calmed the girl somewhat. "Dad sent word out last night to the ranchers hereabouts. They've come with their men. There's the Box-S, the 33-Bar, the Circle-Slash — and the Cross-J — three or four other outfits too. They're mounted and ready —"

"For what?" Johnny cut in sharply.

"They're going raiding. They plan to clean all the nesters out of the valley. Dad says he's going to get rid of them once and for all. The other cowmen are backing him in the movement. We know we're right, even if it is breaking the law. I pleaded with Dad to let you have a try at settling things, but he's lost faith in a law that threatens to take the Cross-J away from him. He wouldn't listen to me. I tried to point out the bloodshed it would bring." The words tumbled frantically from her throat. She went on. "After they've cleaned the valley they plan to move on to Painted Post. Obie Grant will be made prisoner while they work. They're going to round up Ben Cassidy and his gang and run them out, or — or —"

"I know," Johnny said grimly. He stepped back, releasing the girl's shoulders. She hadn't realized how tightly he had been gripping her. Johnny considered. "Maybe it would be no more than justice if I let them go on," he added. "Cassidy and his nest of rattlers need cleaning out. But I don't like to think of what will come later. There'll be more Rangers sent here —"

"Johnny, you've got to stop them! Dad's square. He doesn't realize he's bucking the law. He's just mad clear through. He's not thinking straight. I wasn't either, until yesterday — none of the Cross-J is —"

"I'll do my dangedest!" Johnny promised. He leaped across the room where a holstered six-shooter hung on a wooden peg driven into the wall, examined it, saw it was loaded. On the way back he seized the shotgun Beargrease Jones had left behind, then headed toward the door, stopping momentarily at Pat's side.

"You stay here, Pat —" he commenced.

The girl caught at his sleeve, held his arm. "Johnny," she wailed, "you can't go! I've been a fool. You'll only get yourself killed. Dad's in no mood to be stopped now. Neither are the others. I've never known the Cross-J to be in such an ugly mood. They're angry clear through —"

"That's my outlook," Johnny said swiftly, jerking free of Pat's restraining hands. "I can —"

"You can't do a thing," she said desperately. "You're alone, against so many. They'll kill you if you try to stop them. They won't consider the consequences. Stop! I can't let you go. I shouldn't have asked you —"

But Johnny had already darted through the doorway, six-shooter stuck in the waistband of his trousers, loaded shotgun in his hands. He muttered grimly to himself as he sprinted around the corner of the ranch house, where he could hear the sound made by a body of riders. "They may down me, but I'm betting I won't go down alone!"

XII. Shotgun Law

There weren't any lights shining from the ranch house, but in the light from the stars Johnny Auburn could make out a large body of riders collected and waiting before the long gallery. There must have been fifty mounted men in the group, Johnny figured as he closed in, eying the shadowy forms as he drew near. The horses moved restlessly. Now and then a man swore softly in the night air. Johnny had time to note little more as he drew abreast of the group. He caught the creaking of saddles when the ponies moved; starlight glinted on gun barrels.

Then came Alex Jenkins' voice: "All right, men, we'd better get started. I'm figuring every owner here will be responsible for his own crew. We'll give the scuts a chance. If they're willing to get out peacefully we'll let 'em gather their belongings and go. If they want fight — well, I don't reckon any of us will mind burning a mite of gunpowder on 'em —"

"You'd better hold it, Jenkins!" Johnny called sharply as he drew to a stop before the men, cradling the pointed shotgun in his

121

arms. "I'm figuring to blast the first hombre that touches spurs to his horse!"

For a moment a surprised silence greeted his words; then came Jenkins' wrathful voice: "It's that damned Ranger!"

"How'd you get loose?" Brazos Burnett's voice carried a tone of mingled shock and grudging admiration. "Alex, I swear them knots were tied tight —"

"Never mind how I got loose," Johnny snapped. "All you hombres just use sense and you won't get hurt. Right now my finger is almighty itchy on the trigger, and it wouldn't be wise to startle me none."

Some of the men backed their ponies a few steps. A few raised their arms in the air. The rest, however, appeared more belligerent, and Johnny realized he had his hands full.

Alex Jenkins' wrathful bellow filled the night. "Sit tight, men! Don't let this Ranger bluff you. We got a job to do and, by God, we're going to do it! Auburn, you put down that gun and get to hell out of here. I don't want to see you hurt. I've tried to keep you out of this, but any time a man insists on stepping in front of an express train he's certain to take a bad mangling."

"Sometimes" — Johnny spoke in a steady voice — "the crew of that engine don't get off so easy, neither. There's boards of inquiry, I've heard —"

"Cut the palaver!" a man shouted. "Alex,

are we starting, or aren't we? This country is no place for nesters, and I reckon the same applies to Rangers that insist on cutting into a game that ain't their concern."

"I'm figuring it's my concern plenty," Johnny snapped. "I don't intend to carry on a conversation with anybody but your leader, either, so you can keep your trap shut, hombre. Alex Jenkins, I demand that you give up this move you're planning."

"Demand and be damned!" Jenkins roared. "No Texas Ranger is going to stop us. Men! Is everybody ready to move?"

"Ready and waiting!" went up a score of voices.

"I'm warning you!" Johnny exclaimed. He backed a step, facing the riders, the shotgun in his arms moving in short arcs to cover every man present. "The first man to make a move gets a load of buckshot!"

The riders hesitated now, looking to Jenkins for leadership. Johnny heard Brazos say, "It's up to you, Alex."

"Our move goes through as planned," Jenkins thundered, "Texas Ranger or no Texas Ranger. We've gone too far to stop now — and I ain't intending to stop —"

"Think it over, Jenkins, before you move," Johnny warned. "You and your followers aren't facing just one Texas Ranger — you're facing the whole fighting force, and we don't give up. Sure, you can ride me down if you like, but I'd get one or more of you first. It's up to you to decide if you want that man's — or men's — blood on your hands, Alex Jenkins. For the sake of the argument, we'll say you don't care, though I think you do, if you'll give it a mite of thought. But suppose you do wipe me out. Do you think it will end there? Not by a damned sight! There'll be another Ranger to face, and another and another, until such time as you realize the law can be and will be enforced. I'm talking for your own good and the good of those with you."

"Cripes a'mighty!" Jenkins bellowed. "Cassidy and his kind need to be run out —"

"Maybe I agree with you," Johnny continued, "but that's not your job. That's why the state of Texas organized the Rangers — to take care of lawbusters. Jenkins, you've shown no more sense than a ten-year-old in what you're doing. You're not looking beyond the end of your nose. What's more, you're dragging your neighbors into the mess. As I get it, there's Barr of the 33-Bar; Scott of the Box-S; Fitzherbert of the Circle-Slash — and three or four others. Those men had the foresight to get title to their land. And now you're dragging them into your troubles. They'll be just as guilty as you if they go through with this. And when a man's guilty he always has to pay the law's price when the law catches up with him. What that price might be, I can't say, but it might mean the ruination of your neighbors, Alex Jenkins. Have you thought of that? Do you want it said you ruined your best friends just because you got yourself in a jam? Do you want that on your conscience? And you're due to have it sure as hell, if you insist on this fool plan of yours. Once the Rangers start after you they won't quit. You can't start something and then just laugh it off afterwards."

"Don't pay that Ranger no attention, Alex," a man yelled.

"We're sticking with you, Alex!" from another.

Similar remarks were heard from other men in the crowd. Johnny judged them to be the various ranch owners he'd mentioned. Johnny could feel the cold perspiration standing out on his forehead. He held the riders in check, but how much longer could he hold them? These weren't ordinary crooks to be easily bluffed; these were men who felt their cause was a just one. They'd be just that much harder to convince. At any moment one more excitable than the rest might elect to draw and shoot. When that happened . . . Johnny gulped. He didn't even want to think of it. In the cold light from the stars he could see the grim, relentless faces confronting him. There didn't seem to be any backing down in that direction.

"Come on, Alex," a man cried angrily. "Give the word and we'll ride this Ranger plumb into the earth — the earth that we've fought for — earth that this Ranger would like to see turned over to Cassidy and his snakes —"

"You are a blasted liar!" Johnny's words snapped out with a riflelike velocity. His voice lifted angrily as he decided to throw one last effort into a colossal bluff: "I've stood just about enough from you damned fools, given you more consideration than you're entitled to." His voice fairly smoked with righteous anger. "I'm not going to wait for you hombres to start shooting. I'm going to start it myself!"

He paused to let his words sink in and heard one or two startled gasps from the men ranged before him.

Johnny laughed coldly. "You bunch of fools!" His words were sarcastic, biting, contemptuous. "What ever gave you the idea you could buck the Texas Rangers?" That chilly, scornful laugh again. "I'm counting to three. Cross-J men, head for your corral and unsaddle. The rest of you start your broncs for home. There'll be no raiding of nesters this night. Remember, you've only got until I say 'three.' After that I start pouring lead!"

He tilted the twin barrels of the shotgun a trifle and waited. No one spoke. Johnny said in a clear voice: "One!"

"All right, all right," Alex Jenkins said hastily. "You don't need to count any further, Auburn. I see what you mean. No, I wouldn't want to get my friends in trouble. Charlie, you and the others take your men and drift home. The Cross-J can handle its own problems."

A chorus of voices protested his words. "No, I mean it," Jenkins half shouted. "Get moving! I don't aim to have your blood on my hands just because this damned Ranger has gone crazy. Go on, travel!"

"Two!" Johnny counted inexorably.

There was a sudden breaking up of the knot of riders before him, and the horses moved widely to one side as they were headed toward the roadway. The Cross-J hands sat their ponies stolidly about Alex Jenkins.

"Wouldn't want your own men killed, either, would you, Jenkins?" Johnny queried softly. "Think fast. Time is slipping!"

Jenkins' voice was hard, determined. "My men will keep out of this. This is between you and me, Auburn. I reckon I can handle you alone. You talk about the Rangers sticking to a job. What do you think my men will do? Maybe you can down me, but there's Brazos and all the rest after me. I know my hands. One of them would get you. Now, go ahead" — tauntingly — "give that count of three any time you're ready. I'm waiting for it!"

They faced each other, the Texas Ranger and the old cowman. Johnny stood, half lost in admiration of Jenkins' courage, forgetting momentarily to count, even wondering, when he thought of it, if he could bring himself to voice that fatal "three," wondering if he could draw fast enough to beat the other to the shot and just wound the older man. Even as his lips were forming the word the interruption came.

"Dad!" It was Pat's voice. "Stop it! You can't buck the law. Johnny's made me realize it."

"Pat!" Jenkins said in surprise and then again, a world of sorrow in the single word, "Pat!" He seemed stunned at the girl's intervention, sensing at once she had switched her allegiance to the other side. "Pat, you've let me down."

"No, Dad, no!" Her slim form took shape in the gloom.

Jenkins ignored the girl now. He faced Johnny again. "All right, Ranger Man," he said in dulled tones, "you win. That three count won't be necessary." He climbed stiffly down from the saddle, saying, "Brazos, you and the rest take the broncs back to the corral. That's all for tonight."

They watched him step up on the gallery and head toward the door of the house, his shoulders erect but commencing to slump as he stepped inside.

Johnny started forward. "Mr. Jenkins," he called. Jenkins didn't reply. Johnny pushed his way between the riders. As he passed, Cal Henry caught at his shoulder and held him a moment.

"I'd sure hate to play poker against you," Cal said softly.

Johnny said, "You think I was running a bluff?"

Cal laughed a bit unsteadily. "I'm damned if I know what I think — except you sure got guts, Ranger Man. I'm certain on that."

"All right, boys." Brazos spoke, hard-voiced. "You heard what Alex said. Let's get these broncs unsaddled."

The riders moved off toward the corral. Johnny continued on to the house. As he stepped to the gallery he saw that Pat Jenkins was walking by his side. Neither spoke. He set the shotgun down outside the door and entered the darkened house. Pat said quietly, "I'll light up." He heard a match scratch, and light leaped up in the room.

Alex Jenkins was seated in his big easy chair, head sunk on his chest. He didn't look up at the two standing before him. After a time Pat said, "Dad, listen."

Jenkins raised his head and looked at them. Johnny saw the hurt, bewildered look in his eyes. Like a wounded old buffalo bull was the thought that came to Johnny's mind. All the antagonism and belligerence were gone from Alex Jenkins' face. He was hurt deep down inside. Pat dropped on her knees at her father's side. She put one hand on his arm and said again, "Dad listen to me. Johnny is right —"

That was as far as she got. Jenkins eyed her soberly a moment and then shook his head. "I never figured you'd cross me up this way, Pat."

"But I haven't, Dad. I only did what seemed right to do. We can't go counterwise of the law. It was all for your own good. Johnny thinks maybe he can work this whole thing out."

"So it's 'Johnny' now, eh?" Jenkins said bitterly. "You used to call him 'that Ranger,' or 'Auburn.' It's no secret to me now, how he got loose."

"Don't jump to conclusions, Mr. Jenkins," Johnny cut in. "I'd found a way to cut those rawhides. I'd been loose anyway, I figure, in time —"

"I don't want it that way, Johnny," Pat said defiantly. "Yes, Dad, I cut the rawhides, told him what you were planning. But your way wasn't the right way. If you'll only let Johnny handle things, maybe —"

"Maybe!" Jenkins snorted, regaining some of his old spirit. "My way was *sure!*"

"If you'd just listen to me," Pat persisted.

"I'll listen," the old man growled. "What's your plan, Auburn? — not that I got any faith in it."

"That's something I can't tell you now," Johnny explained. "I haven't got it all worked out yet. You'll just have to take my word that I'm on your side and agree to keep hands off."

"In other words," Jenkins said savagely, "you want me to admit I'm licked. You want me to promise that I won't take any further action against Cassidy and the damn hoe men. You want me to sit back and watch those coyotes string wire back and forth across my valley until it's all tangled up like a ball of twine and a kitten. You want to be able to report to your blasted Ranger headquarters that you've settled the trouble here —"

"Yes sir," Johnny said eagerly, "that's exactly what I do want — though I wouldn't say yet you were licked."

"What else can you call it?" Jenkins' voice was bitter. "My own daughter has swung to your side. Why should I fight any longer? All right, I admit it. I'm licked. The Cross-J that I built up with my own hands and Pat's mother's is to be turned over to a bunch of thieving scoundrels. You win, Auburn. I won't make any more trouble over this valley without I've got your go-ahead — and I don't see myself getting that."

"I've got your word on it?" Johnny insisted.

"My word is as good as yours," Jenkins said brokenly. "That's all I have got left —"

"No, Dad, no," Pat protested.

"You've got my word on it," Jenkins told Johnny. "I hope you didn't expect me to shake on it too."

Johnny smiled thinly. "Not yet, I don't," he said cryptically, nodded good night to Pat, and headed for the bunkhouse.

In the bunkhouse he found a somber crew sitting around and talking little. Their eyes were far from friendly when Johnny entered. Johnny said, "Nice little party we had to-night."

"Was it?" Brazos growled. "From my standpoint it was pretty lousy."

Johnny smiled, sat down on his bunk, and commenced taking off his boots. "Maybe you'll change your standpoint one of these days, Brazos."

"If so, I'll be surprised," Brazos snapped. "And, furthermore, I'm not sure if we want you sleeping here with us tonight."

"That so?" Johnny said mildly. "You must have changed your mind. You were all plumb anxious to keep me in this bunk a spell back."

Anger struggled with curiosity in Brazos' features. "All right," he said begrudgingly, "it's your bunk for the night."

Johnny said in a light tone, "Thanks."

Brazos reddened, then asked, "It was Pat that cut you loose, wa'n't it?"

Johnny evaded that one. He said, "Come

here. . . . See this sharp edge of wood where a knot fell out? Well, with a mite of patience a feller could saw a rawhide through on that, I'm betting. Course it would take time."

Brazos exploded, "Well, I'll be damned!"

"We'll all be," Hub Fanning grouched, "if we have to have a Ranger around here all the time."

Johnny faced the men, grinning. "All right. You're sore. Maybe I don't blame you. But you've got to admit I was only doing a job I was sent here to do. Sure, you all hate me like poison —"

"Why shouldn't we?" Yank Ferguson demanded. "You're turning this whole valley over to Cassidy and his skunks."

"That," Johnny denied, "is something yet to be proved. Maybe you'll change your tune later. Meanwhile, I'd appreciate it a heap if you'd all shut up and let me get to sleep. I've had a hard day."

"*You've* had a hard day?" Cal Henry cut in. "What do you think we've been doing, tripping the light fantastic on the greensward?"

"It's my bet you all tripped on something," Johnny chuckled. And, rolling into blankets, Johnny, for the second time that night, gave vent to a distinct sigh of relief. After considerable disgruntled muttering the rest of the crew crawled into bunks.

XIII. No Quitter

The crew was even less friendly the following morning. By this time they'd had an opportunity to think over how Johnny had faced them down. They felt he was turning the Cross-J over to the Cassidy gang, and the thought irked them considerably. On this morning there'd been no invitation for Johnny to eat at the ranch house with Jenkins and his daughter; however, the unwritten law of the range insisted that Johnny be given his breakfast, even though the men's faces showed that Johnny was far from welcome.

He ate in silence. When he was nearly through Brazos Burnett entered the bunkhouse, bearing Johnny's belt and gun. "Here's your armament, Auburn," he said shortly. "Any time you get ready to leave is all right with us."

"I'd like to run up to the house a minute," Johnny commenced.

"There ain't any need. Alex don't want to talk to you. He's passed his word; there'll be no more fighting the nesters unless you say so. That ends the matter. Oh yes, you have a bronc to get to Painted Post. Just leave it at the Alamo Livery. We'll pick it up later."

Johnny put down his coffee cup and rose from the table. "I reckon if you're feeling that way," he said coldly, "I don't want to borrow your pony. I can make to walk to town —"

"Now, look here, Ranger Man," Brazos started, his bronzed face flushing, "we aim to do what's right. We ain't making anybody walk —"

"Cut it." Johnny laughed frigidly. "Seeing you all feel the way you do, I wouldn't want to be under obligations." He rose, strapped on his belt and gun, put on his sombrero, and started for the doorway. At the exit he paused, looked back at the men seated at the table. "I reckon I know how you feel. I can even understand it. Right now there ain't a man among you that doesn't hate me — for doing my duty. That's all right with me. Maybe you'll change your mind eventually. *Adiós!*" And he stepped outside.

For a moment there was silence at the table; then Cal Henry, looking defiantly at the rest, rose and hurried to the doorway. "Hey, Auburn," he called, "you can have my pony."

Johnny paused and looked around, grinning. "Thanks just the same, Cal. I appreciate that. But I'll walk. You have to live with that crew of sourpusses in there. They'd

135

make it tough if I took your horse. Maybe I'll see you in town — or out here. I'm coming back, you know. Sure as hell I'm coming back, whether the Cross-J likes it or not."

He continued on his way, walking with a long easy stride that he knew, in his heart, wouldn't last long. High-heeled riding boots, were never made to walk in. He'd probably have blisters before long. But even that thought didn't stop the cheerful whistle that rose to his lips.

Back in the bunkhouse, the men watched Cal Henry reenter. Cal eyed them belligerently. Sheepish, embarrassed looks commenced to creep into their faces. Yank Ferguson said, "What do you suppose Auburn meant when he said he was coming back — whether we like it or not?"

"I don't know and I don't give a damn!" Cal said angrily. "I hope he does. I hope he arrests every mother's son here. We're a bunch of soreheads if you ask me, ashamed to admit that he licked us singlehanded last night. Whether you like him or not, you got to admit he's just about the biggest chunk of courage we've ever seen wrapped in one bundle. The idea, him walking to town —"

"I told him he could have a horse," Brazos said defensively.

Cal turned angrily on the speaker. "And how did you tell him?" he snarled. "You tried to make him feel like he was dirt around here. By Gawd! I've heard a lot about Texas hospitality, but this is a new kind, it seems to me. We abduct a man, and then because he licks us seven ways from the ace we force him to walk back to town. Me, I'm not craving to work for any outfit that cheap. I'm getting out. Brazos, you can leave my wages at the Cash Deal next time you come to town. I don't want to work around here any longer."

"Maybe we'll be glad to see you go," Jiggs Monahan exclaimed, losing his temper. "Any puncher that crosses up his own outfit for a lousy two-bit Texas Ranger —"

"You ain't telling me I crossed up this outfit!" Cal said wrathfully and started for the speaker. Monahan saw it coming and quickly stepped back from the table.

The two men met with arms flailing wildly. Both connected. Before second blows could be struck Brazos and a couple of other punchers separated them. Brazos was cursing wildly by this time, his own temper torn to shreds. Instantly the bunkhouse was filled with excited voices. Things finally quieted down.

"You, Cal," Brazos said, "maybe I can't blame you for acting like you did. Jiggs never had no call to say you double-crossed the outfit. At the same time, you got to admit you sided that Ranger."

"I sure did." Cal brushed one hand across a rapidly swelling cheekbone. "I also announced I was getting out."

"There ain't no need for that," Brazos said. "We're all mighty hair-triggered this morning. We'd better settle down and be friends."

"Not me," Cal said stubbornly. "I'm leaving, and I hope when Auburn does come back he makes you eat your words and your thoughts about him — every damn one of 'em. The feller had a job to do. He outbluffed us and did it. It's the first time I ever knew the Cross-J to object to law-enforcing. That being the case, it's time I got out before I get into any more fights."

They watched him roll his stuff into blankets in silence. After a few minutes he nodded coldly and left the bunkhouse. The rest dropped dejectedly into chairs.

Meanwhile, Johnny had continued on his way and was just passing the long gallery at the front of the house when he heard Pat Jenkins' voice. The girl came down from the porch to ask him where he was going.

"Painted Post. How's your dad feel this morning?"

The girl looked serious. "Dad has taken it all pretty hard, Johnny. I've told him to try giving you a chance, but he doesn't trust anyone — now that he thinks I've turned against him. He scarcely answers when I speak to him —" She broke off suddenly to say, "Did you say Painted Post? You're not walking!"

Johnny grinned cheerfully. "I always take a long walk mornings. It's good for the constitution."

"Johnny! What happened down in the bunkhouse?"

"Nothing that need concern you."

"But it does concern me! Johnny, did Brazos get ugly?"

"I wouldn't say so."

"He did; I know he did. He sent you away without a horse. Dad won't like that — even if —"

"You're wrong, Pat. He offered me a bronc to get to town on. I just didn't feel like accepting."

"Maybe I can understand that too. You wait here."

"Now wait a minute, Pat —"

But it was no use. The girl had already turned and was running toward the bunkhouse. Johnny looked after her regretfully, then decided it was no use to stay for further arguments. Resuming his whistle, he started along the well-traveled roadway that ran to Painted Post.

At the end of twenty minutes Johnny's boots had commenced to bind. He knew another twenty minutes would produce a nice crop of blisters. He slowed pace somewhat, chuckling ruefully to himself: "Let this be a lesson to you, Johnny Auburn. Sometimes it doesn't pay to be too damn independent. Cripes! It would be such a nice morning for riding too. Not a cloud in the sky. Nice timbered hills on both sides of this valley. Golly, I'll bet there's post oak and cypress up there that ain't ever felt the touch of a human. Just cows and coyotes and rabbits. This is sure nice country. I could do with a few friends, though. If my plans don't work out, that Patricia girl won't ever speak to me again — let alone the Cross-J cow hands and Alex Jenkins. And I sure don't crave to be on friendly terms with Cassidy and his skunks. Cripes all fishhooks! There must be some way of breaking those leases that Cassidy got for his nester friends, but I'm danged if I see how yet." He winced suddenly as a burning sensation occurred in the region of his right heel. "There's a blister," he told himself ruefully. "Reckon it might help if I switched my socks."

He dropped down at the side of the trail in the shadow of a mesquite and drew off his boots. At that moment, glancing back toward the Cross-J, he saw a cloud of dust approaching. The cloud dissolved, and Johnny saw that the rider was Cal Henry. Cal was leading a second horse. "Cal, you're sure welcome if that bronc is for me," Johnny told himself.

The rider drew abreast and stopped. Cal's

lips twitched as he noted Johnny sitting in his sock feet. "What's up, Ranger Man, your pedal extremities fretting you a mite?"

"More'n a mite." Johnny grinned up at him. "That bronc you're leading wouldn't be for me, would it?"

"According to Pat, it is."

"That's Pat's horse?"

Cal nodded. "We both hit the corral and started saddling up about the same time. I figured to take you up behind me, but she insisted on me taking her horse for you. Far be it from me to argify with a lady. I never yet won an argument with a girl. My system has always been to never let 'em start talking. Or weeping. There ain't a thing in the world to be done when they turn on the weeps but just give in."

Johnny looked surprised. "Pat wasn't crying?"

"Not her," Cal said scornfully. "The Cross-J hands may be by this time, though. When I rode past the bunkhouse with this extra horse I could sure hear her giving Brazos and the rest their comeuppance. Pat was sure laying 'em out with as pretty a tongue lashing as you'd want to hear. A verbal flaying, you might call it. That girl can put more meaning into a statement, without downright cussing, than any girl I ever see."

While he talked Johnny had been putting on his boots. Now he rose and got into the saddle of Pat's horse. Cal relinquished the reins to him. "I lengthened them stirrup leathers to what I figured was about right," Cal said.

"They're fine." Johnny nodded. "Thank Pat for me when you go back."

"Ain't going back," Cal said. "I done quit the outfit."

"Not on my account, I hope."

"On my own. I could have stayed."

Johnny guessed something of what had happened, but he didn't say anything more, knowing that Cal wouldn't wish him to. Now for the first time Johnny noticed the swollen right cheekbone on Cal's face. He said dryly, "Apparently you had a mite of trouble when you quit."

"No trouble for me," Cal said airily. "I was just going good when they stopped it. C'mon, you riding to Painted Post?"

They rode on for a half-hour, with Cal keeping up a continual chatter. By this time Johnny had his man pretty well sized up. He sensed that Cal had hated to quit the Cross-J; only Cal's rigid sense of justice had promoted his act. Once the hot words had left his lips he had had to go through with it.

Johnny asked suddenly, "How long you been with the Cross-J?"

Cal sobered. "Gosh, I don't just remember. It's the only outfit I ever worked for. Alex Jenkins took me in when I was a small button. You see, my folks died early and — Y'know, I hope Alex won't feel bad about me quitting this way. I'll see him in town, after things quiet down, and try to explain my stand to him. I reckon I can make him see it my way. Alex has always been right square."

"I guessed that much. Where do you figure to work next?"

Cal shrugged. "I'll stick around Painted Post until somebody brings in my wages. Then I'll light out and find a job someplace. No use me trying at any of the spreads hereabouts. None of 'em would take on a hombre that had quit Alex Jenkins. Hands just don't quit a man like that —"

"Maybe you acted too impulsively."

"I'm danged if I did."

"Like to work for the Cross-J again, wouldn't you?"

Cal gulped. "Yeah, I sure would — if things were different."

Johnny nodded. "Maybe you will. Meanwhile, if you want a job, maybe you can do something for me. I'll pay as good as you've been getting and expense money —"

"You mean I'd be a Ranger?"

Johnny shook his head. "This is something else, something you'd have to keep secret. I'm resigning from the Rangers, Cal. Keep that under your hat."

"T'hell you are!" Cal Henry's features expressed extreme amazement. "What's the idea?"

"Keep that secret now. I'm announcing that fact to no one, except headquarters, for a while. I'm trusting you to keep still."

"You can trust me. But I don't understand."

"It's this way, Cal," Johnny explained quietly. "I came here with a job to do for the Rangers. It was up to me to make Alex Jenkins quit bucking the law. Alex has admitted he's licked. He's passed his word that he won't kick up any more fuss, cut any more wire, without my say-so. His word is good enough for me. My job is done, and I can wire my captain to that effect —"

"But why the resignation now?"

Johnny smiled wryly. "It was a mighty distasteful job, Cal. My sympathies were with the Cross-J all the way through, but I'd sworn to enforce the law. I couldn't do anything else. I hate Ben Cassidy and his gang worse'n poison, but they had law on their side, regardless what you say. I enforced that law. Now I'm leaving the Rangers, so I can throw in with the Cross-J and lick hell out of the Cassidy gang."

"Johnny!" Cal's face lighted with enthusiasm.

"That's the way it is." Johnny nodded. "I've found that every so often the enforcing of the law doesn't bring justice to the right

144

parties. Ethically, I think Alex Jenkins is entitled to keep his land. Legally, he isn't. I'm going to find a way to fix it for him legally."

"Whoopee-ee-e!" Cal let out a sudden cowboy yell that startled a jack rabbit out of the brush at the side of the road. Then his face fell suddenly. "But, Johnny, how you going to do it?"

"I'm not sure yet," Johnny said slowly, "but I've a hunch I can work things out."

"Even if it meant bucking the law yourself?" Cal asked swiftly.

Johnny nodded determinedly. "I haven't forgotten how the Cross-J crew looked this morning. Hell! I know how they all felt. But we're going to go slow, Cal, until I can get my ideas organized. So far as anybody else is concerned, I'll still be a Texas Ranger for the present. Are you with me?"

"Until hell freezes over!" he said fervently.

"Good. In the first place, clear title can't be had for the Cross-J until the land has been surveyed. Here's what I want you to do. When we get to Painted Post I've some letters to write; then I want you to go to Fritada, catch the train to Austin, and mail my letters. While in Austin you're to look up a surveyor for me, whose name I'll give you, and arrange for him to come and bring his crew —"

"Wait a minute," Cal cut in, frowning. "I think the Cross-J was surveyed one time. I remember hearing about it when I was a kid, seems like."

"Did Jenkins have the land surveyed?"

Cal shook his head. "No, I have a feeling it was some sort of state project. I know one time the authorities were going to have all Texas surveyed, but the idea was dropped. I don't know why, but I do know Alex didn't have it done. I got the story from an old freighter that used to come through here. Somehow, I seem to remember vaguely that he said Alex was away at the time. I never paid much attention to the story, anyway. As I got it, this freighter used to bring in a beef animal, all slaughtered, for the surveying crew now and then. You don't think that Alex would have title to the land just because it was surveyed?"

Johnny shook his head. "No, but if this land ever has been surveyed it will make my job that much easier. But we'll have the matter checked, to make sure. I'll give you a note to this surveyor, and he can look up the records at the land office for me, then bring a crew here to do what's necessary."

"Then what?"

Johnny said slowly, "I'm not sure yet. We'll cross that bridge when we come to it, Cal. C'mon, let's get to Painted Post. All this talking has made my throat mighty dry."

Cal frowned and shook his head. "I still can't believe you're quitting the Rangers —

figuring to go against all they stand for —"

"Don't get that idea." Johnny smiled. "And I'm not quitting. Cowboy, I'm just starting!"

XIV. A Miscarriage of Justice

Sheriff Obie Grant was seated at his roll-top desk in the office when Johnny entered. Hearing the step in the doorway, Obie pushed a sorrowful, worry-ridden face around the corner of the desk to see who was entering. His features quickly took on an expression of amazement, then gladness, as he leaped up and started to pump Johnny's hand.

"Johnny! Johnny Auburn!" he exclaimed. "I was commencing to think mebbe you were dead."

"Not me." Johnny laughed, rounding the desk and finding a chair close to Obie's.

"Where in hell you been? What happened to you? You caused me a lot of trouble."

Johnny grinned. "I heard something of that — out to the Cross-J."

"Cripes a'mighty! You been to the Cross-J all this time? Whyn't you say you were going? How'd you get there? Your horse was still in the livery. You must have left plumb sudden. If you'd only've told me —"

"Whoa! whoa!" Johnny laughed. "Circumstances beyond my control prevented me letting you know. . . ." From that point on Johnny continued and told Obie what had happened, while Obie's eyes grew wider and wider and his lower jaw went slack. Johnny left out only that part pertaining to his contemplated resignation from the Rangers.

"Why, damn that Cal Henry!" Obie exclaimed indignantly. "He was in here the day after you was abducted. I asked him if he'd seen you and he said no."

"Put yourself in Cal's place," Johnny reminded. "You'd have done the same thing. I left Cal down to the Cash Deal — just stopped for one drink before coming here. I got some letters to write, if you'll let me use your desk."

"Take it and welcome." Obie's face darkened. "You know what? That damn Cassidy is planning to sue me for false arrest."

"I heard about that too. Maybe I can persuade him otherwise."

Obie brightened, then looked sober again. "In a way you ran a heap of risk facing down Alex Jenkins and his crowd. I don't know but what it would have been safer — and better all around — to just let Alex wipe out all the nesters, including Cassidy. That might have settled the trouble."

Johnny shook his head. "Alex and his men could have done it all right, but they'd just found themselves in more trouble. It was from that I was trying to save 'em. If they'd

149

gone through with that plan it would have been necessary to arrest every man jack of 'em. I didn't want to do that. I want Alex to get legal right to his property."

"Too late for that now, I reckon," Obie said moodily. "Now that you've got Alex stopped, Cassidy and his crowd will just fence off the whole Painted Post Valley. Johnny, you've managed to enforce the law, but you've also managed to knock the props from under the best cowman that ever lived. It will be hard for him and Pat to have to leave the Cross-J." His face flushed angrily. "Damn all law anyway!"

"Don't take that attitude, Obie," Johnny advised quietly. "Just between you and me — and don't let this go any farther — I'm aiming to see if things can't be worked out so Alex can keep his land."

"I don't know how you're going to do it," Obie growled.

"I'm not sure yet either, but I've got hopes."

Obie shook his head. "If only Alex had got title, or even paid taxes on the Cross-J. One thing I do know; I know he paid taxes on a dang big herd of cows years after year —"

"That's not land taxes."

Obie sighed. "I suppose not. I reckon Alex must have figured he'd done everything needed when he paid his cattle tax."

"Mebbe so," Johnny said absent-mindedly.

"By the way, Obie, there's no need of you mentioning it was the Cross-J that abducted me that night. We don't want to give Cassidy and his gang anything to crow about."

Obie's face fell. "All right, if you say so, but I'm sure craving to ride those Cross-J hands about the way you turned the tables on 'em. It would sort of even up for that ten-dollar bet I lost to Cassidy — the skunk. Lucky for me, I made that ten up, though; I was looking through the pigeonholes in this desk yesterday and I found a ten-dollar bill stuck in one of 'em. So I'm not out anything."

"Except a mite of ribbing." Johnny smiled. "Just between you and me, Obie, Cal Henry left that bill there. The boys on the Cross-J didn't want you to lose any money through their doings, so they took up a collection and —"

"T'hell you say! Well, that's mighty white of 'em. . . . That damn Cassidy, though, he like to make me boiling mad with his actions. After he got my ten he went over to Smith's General Store and bought a new ring and a neckerchief — even bought new ca'tridges and tossed his old ones at my feet, saying the county would need donations." He gestured toward a tumbled heap of cartridges at one corner of his desk. "If it wa'n't that they're N.E.P. ca'tridges and not worth a whoop I'd be plumb inclined to load with 'em, in the

151

hope of using one of 'em to let daylight through Ben Cassidy."

Johnny picked up a couple of the cartridges and examined them. His face looked thoughtful. After a time he rolled the loads back on Obie's desk with the words, "Take care of those, Obie. We may need 'em."

"Meaning what?" Obie asked curiously.

"I'll tell you when I think it over. Just hang onto 'em."

Obie shrugged. "Just as you say."

Johnny asked next, "Say, did anybody from the Cross-J bring in a body yesterday morning?"

"Pearly Gates!" Obie exploded. "In the excitement at seeing you back I'd plumb forgot. Yeah, Yank Ferguson and Jiggs Monahan brought him in real early. They claimed Pearly was throwing lead promiscuous around there night before last, and he got his comeuppance. They refused to say who done it. Since then Ben Cassidy has been making life miserable for me, insisting that I arrest the whole Cross-J crowd — though he insists that Pearly wa'n't a personal friend of him. What do you know about it?"

"I shot him," Johnny said soberly. "He wasn't alone. The other dry-gulcher got away. They both opened fire just as I was stepping out the back door of the ranch house. I made a lucky shot, and Gates stayed where he dropped."

152

Obie looked relieved. "I wish you'd explain that to Cassidy. In your capacity of Texas Ranger you were acting within your rights."

"I'll explain to Cassidy all right," Johnny said grimly. "There's a lot I aim to explain to that hombre before I get through with him. Right now, Obie, I've got some letters to write. If you don't mind letting me use your desk —"

"Help yourself." Obie rose. "You'll find pen and ink, paper and envelopes handy. I'll drift down to the Cash Deal and see if I can't persuade Cal Henry to buy me a drink. Gawd knows, after all the misery he's caused me, I'm entitled to one."

Johnny seated himself at the desk when Obie had departed and quickly wrote two letters. The letter of resignation to Captain Travis consumed more thought; after several false starts he finally made a beginning, explaining in detail what had been accomplished, then continuing:

The job you sent me here to do is finished, and I think you can safely inform the governor that there is no need of soldiers or another Texas Ranger being sent here in the immediate future. I use "another" advisedly: while I expect to stay on here for a time, I am taking this opportunity to resign from the Texas Rangers, with your kind permission, rather than reenlist next week, at which time my present period of service ends. This is a move I have long contemplated, as you know. The truth is, Captain Travis, I'm not sure but that justice has miscarried in the case of Alex Jenkins, and my conscience refuses to let me leave here until I have at least endeavored to right matters. This may involve steps I couldn't honestly take as a member of the Texas Rangers, though rest assured I shall not do anything contrary to the law of our state. Meanwhile, there is a very capable sheriff located in Painted Post. He is well fitted to handle any contingencies that may arise, so there is small need for you to worry about any fresh outbreak of hostilities requiring Ranger intervention in this locality.

Johnny added a few more miscellaneous remarks and closed with:

I remain, sir, your sincere friend and associate of many enjoyable days,
JOHN AUBURN

The letter finished, Johnny addressed an envelope, thrust the sheets of paper inside, and sealed them. Then, rising, he walked out to the street and headed in the direction of the Cash Deal Saloon, where he found Obie

Grant and Cal Henry talking over glasses of beer. Obie returned to his office after a few minutes, and Johnny passed his letters over to Cal, saying, "If you'll leave now, I think you can reach Fritada in time to catch the Texas & Pacific for Fort Worth. You change there for Austin. Mail this letter to Captain Travis at Fort Worth. This second letter is to the surveyor I mentioned. Deliver that in person. You'll probably find him around the land office at the capital, or somebody there can tell you his whereabouts. This third letter is also to be mailed at Fort Worth. It's to my bank in San Antonio."

He watched Cal leave and mount his pony for the ride to Fritada, then called after him, "Tell that station agent at Fritada that Cherokee is now able to write my letters for me."

Frowning, Cal turned in the saddle. "Cherokee?"

"My pony." Johnny laughed.

Cal said, "You don't make sense."

"The stationman will know what I mean."

Cal nodded and rode on. Johnny looked after him for a time, then turned his steps toward the Maverick Saloon, the sign of which he had noticed about a block down the street on the opposite side. "Probably I can find Ben Cassidy there as quick as any place," he mused. "It's about time Ben and I renewed acquaintances, I reckon."

Cassidy, Malotte, and Tascosa Jake were

155

standing at the far end of the bar, heads bent in close consultation, when Johnny entered the Maverick. Louie, the barkeep, was engaged in serving a small group nearer the front. These men may have been farmers, though Johnny noticed they all carried six-shooters. He didn't at all like their appearance.

Cassidy happened to look up as Johnny entered. His features stiffened; then he forced a look of pleased surprise and hastened to greet Johnny: "Well, well, if it isn't my old friend, Ranger Auburn. Long time no see, Johnny." He stretched out one hand.

Johnny was engaged in rolling a cigarette and pretended not to see the hand offered him. He nodded easily. "Didn't know you considered yourself such a friend of mine, Cassidy. Seems like I remember you avoiding me as much as possible back in those Santa Angela days."

"Hell, I never had any fuss with you." Cassidy laughed. "Lot of folks had it in for me 'bout that time, remember? Feller pulled a gun on me and I had to shoot him. Hated like hell to do it, but it was him or me. Then his friends tried to get me hung for murder, but the facts were clear; it was pure self-defense."

Johnny nodded. "I remember the jury bringing in a verdict to that effect. No, I didn't have anything to do with that case."

Cassidy was anxious to change the subject.

"Come on over here; meet a couple of friends of mine, Cold-Deck Malotte and Tascosa Jake Wiley."

Johnny followed the man to the bar and nodded to the two.

Malotte said, "Pleased to meet any friend of Ben's." He put out one hand which Johnny failed to see. Tascosa made no effort to shake hands, nor did he assume anything but an appearance of antagonism. His nod was as short as Johnny's.

"What you drinking?" Cassidy invited.

"Nothing right now," Johnny refused.

"You know" — Cassidy laughed genially — "you had this town all upset for a spell. I was plumb worried about you. We heard you arrived in Painted Post; then all of a sudden you disappeared. That fool, Obie Grant, even arrested me for your murder, or something of the kind. Course he couldn't make it stick. I'm figuring to sue the county for false arrest —"

"Don't try it, Cassidy," Johnny said quietly, and added what was pure bluff. "You'd better check into the law a mite. Obie was within his rights, even if he himself didn't know it at the time."

"That right?" Cassidy frowned. "I didn't realize that. You sure?"

"Where a Texas Ranger is concerned, the law is different in some ways," Johnny said smoothly.

Carelessly Cassidy nodded. "We'll let it drop. I note you're not wearing a Ranger badge."

"Didn't figure it necessary," Johnny replied. "Folks in Texas know me pretty well by this time. I can produce a badge if you'd like to see it."

"Not me," Cassidy said hastily. "Sure you don't want a drink?"

"Dead sure. By the way, what you doing around here, Ben?"

"Nothing much," Cassidy replied readily. "Dropped in to see my old friend, Cold-Deck. Then I sort of got interested in these farmers that have taken out leases hereabouts. They weren't getting a square deal from the Cross-J and I've been — well, sort of advising them. Just which side you taking, Johnny?"

"The law's," Johnny said bleakly.

Cassidy looked uneasy. "That means, then, that you'll stop the Cross-J from cutting the farmers' wire and killing — ?"

"It's already stopped," Johnny cut in. "I've talked it over with Alex Jenkins. He sees things my way. There'll be no more wire cut without my say-so."

"Why — why, that's fine." Cassidy was surprised and puzzled. The victory was easier than he had expected. "You say you've seen Jenkins?"

Johnny said impatiently, "Where do you

158

think I've been the past few days?"

"You been to the Cross-J all this time? Wonder you wouldn't let your friends know where you're going. We all thought there'd been some dirty work."

"Not where I was concerned," Johnny said quietly, "though there was some tried night before last. Feller named Pearly Gates tried to dry-gulch me. I understand you've been trying to force Obie Grant to make an arrest at the Cross-J. You can forget that, Cassidy. I did that killing. I'm responsible. From the fuss you've been kicking up, I judge Gates must have been a pal of yours."

"Hell, no!" Cassidy protested. "I just wanted to see justice done, was all. I just knew Gates to speak to."

Johnny turned suddenly on Tascosa. "You're not looking any too happy, Wiley. Was Gates a friend of yours?"

"If he was," Tascosa rasped angrily, "I might be out to get the hombre that finished him."

Johnny smiled thinly. "Good thing he wasn't a friend of yours, then. It might be bad for you. Gates had a friend with him, but the lousy two-bit, no-good skunk made a fast getaway."

"Why, damn you, Auburn!" Tascosa snarled. "If you're saying I was with Pearly that night —"

"Tascosa!" Cassidy snapped. "You shut up.

159

Johnny ain't insinuating anything of the sort. Tascosa's too hot-tempered," Cassidy added to Johnny.

"Yeah, looks that-a-way, doesn't it?" Johnny agreed carelessly. He smiled contemptuously at Tascosa, hoping to goad the man to direct action, but Tascosa maintained a sullen silence.

To change the subject Cassidy called down the bar to the group of farmerish-looking individuals standing there: "I've got good news, boys. Ranger Auburn promises there'll be no more fence-cutting. He's stopped the Cross-J cold."

The group brightened at the words, though one of the men said sulkily, "It's about time we got some justice."

Johnny ignored the man and turned back to Cassidy. "Just how did your men go about choosing their places, Cassidy? What do their leases call for?"

Cassidy shrugged. "I don't know exactly. I've never gone into the matter much. And they're not my men. To hear you talk, you'd think I'd brought them here."

"Didn't you?" Johnny asked smoothly.

"Certainly not. Cripes! I don't know much about their leases. They got papers calling for certain pieces of land, and when they started fencing, the Cross-J —"

"I know about that part," Johnny interrupted. "What I'm getting at, did these farmers have their places surveyed?"

"Hell! Why should they? There's plenty of land. They just paced off the distances their papers called for." Cassidy frowned. "Isn't that all right?"

Johnny shook his head. "How do you ever expect them to avoid trouble over property lines? Let one of those farmers take in more of Alex Jenkins' property than he should and you'll hear an almighty yelp out of Jenkins. I figured that's about what happened. Well, I've sent for a surveyor to come here and get measurements right."

"Hell! These fellers haven't any money for surveyors," Cassidy protested. He commenced to look uneasy.

"Did I say they needed any money?"

"Oh." Cassidy's face cleared. "You mean the state pays for the surveying costs."

"The surveying won't cost your men a cent," Johnny said easily. "Just make sure they have their papers in order when I call for 'em."

"I can do that," Cassidy said readily.

Johnny nodded. "That's all then. I reckon we understand each other. See you again, Cassidy." He nodded and left the saloon, not bothering to speak to Malotte or Tascosa.

The instant he had left Cassidy burst out laughing. "All my worrying for nothing," he chuckled. "Hell's bells! The Ranger is on our side."

Tascosa sneered. "And once we've got out of him all we need I'm sure going to plug that son. Cripes! He don't look tough to me."

Cassidy smiled confidently. "I reckon he has tamed down a heap. I'm damned if I ever expected to see him so agreeable. But I'm not forgetting Pearly Gates, neither. When this business is settled to our liking Mister Ranger Auburn is due to stop a slug of lead!"

XV. The Buzzards Gather

Two days passed in which Johnny did little more than stay around Painted Post, getting acquainted with the various leading citizens and dropping into Urban Everett's Cash Deal Saloon, where he enjoyed both the creamy beer and the conversation of the genial proprietor and mayor of the town. Of Ben Cassidy, Johnny had seen nothing, though, for all he knew, Cassidy might have been spending his time at the Maverick Saloon.

On the third day the surveyor, Sam Blaine, arrived. Johnny was seated in a tilted-back chair on the porch of the Cash Deal Saloon when he saw Blaine and Cal Henry riding their dusty ponies into Painted Post. He hailed them, and they drew to a stop as he got to his feet.

"Hi-yuh Johnny," Cal said. "Made pretty good time, didn't we? I'll take Mr. Blaine's bronc on down to the livery. His throat is probably too dusty to travel any farther."

Blaine got down and came up to the porch while Cal went on with the two horses. Sam Blaine was a man past middle age, with iron-gray hair, sharp-piercing eyes, and a lean, tough frame. He shook hands enthusiastically. "It's good to see you again, Johnny."

"That works both ways."

Blaine knocked the dust from his sombrero and seated himself on a chair next to Johnny's while Johnny entered the saloon, to emerge a moment later with two cold bottles of beer. After a few minutes the two got down to business.

"Your man Cal had a time locating me," Blaine was explaining. "I've left the land office and gone freelancing on my own. With my commission from the state I'm in line to make a good thing of it, I believe —"

Johnny cut in, "You are going to take over the surveying job for me, aren't you? I didn't see your crew and —"

"They're on the way," Blaine explained. "They stopped in Fritada to pick up a wagon and some horses. We weren't sure what we could get in Painted Post, so thought we'd better do business there, rather than have to go back if Painted Post couldn't furnish the necessary. Oh yes, we've got the equipment, and I have my regular chain carriers and flagmen along. Even brought my own cook for the job."

"How long do you figure it will take?" Johnny asked. "Cal had an impression that the state had, at one time, surveyed Painted Post Valley."

"I know he did." Blaine nodded. "When he

couldn't locate me right away he tried to find something in the records about it himself. Didn't have any luck, and nobody in the land office could help him. They didn't know where to look. There's a new gang in there since my time. Cal finally located me, and I knew just what file to look in."

"The valley has been surveyed then?"

Blaine nodded. "Long time back. The state of Texas didn't do it, though. Sam Houston did. As I got the story, old Sam saw the valley and liked it, decided to have it surveyed and then buy it as a present for his nephew, Jesse Chisholm, as a sort of recognition of Jess' services to this country in opening the Chisholm Trail."

"You say Chisholm was Houston's nephew? He was part Cherokee Indian, wasn't he?"

"Nephew by marriage. Old Sam married a Cherokee woman, you know. Anyway, Sam died shortly after he left the U.S. Senate, and the idea fell through, though the survey was made, but no deed was ever recorded. So the valley is on the state records as open range. I don't know whether Chisholm ever did anything about it or not. He died three or four years after Sam, from eating too much bear meat that had been left in a brass kettle overnight. Leastwise that's the story as I heard it."

Johnny looked thoughtful. "If a survey was made, it shouldn't take you long to check up on boundary lines, corners and so on."

"I shouldn't think so either, Johnny. According to the papers I brought with me, Sam Houston's surveyors established their corner, or commencement point, all right. It's supposed to be up near the head of the Rio Pinto — a stake buried in charcoal near a hatchet-shaped outcropping of red sandstone. Several post oaks and one big pin oak were notched to help establish the legal corner. Once we've located that, I can run my lines and check in on the various other points. As a matter of fact, I'm not sure my services are actually needed. You might be able to take these old records of Sam Houston's surveyors and —"

"I'd rather have a complete check on 'em. Trees fall or are cut down. Sometimes corners are established in sand hills; after a number of years the hills shift in the wind. No, what I want, Sam, is a complete check that can be taken into court, if necessary. Old records are too easy to break down sometimes. And if anybody asks you any questions as to what you're doing, just refer 'em to me. Don't talk to strangers, understand?"

Blaine frowned. "Why all the secrecy, Johnny? What's going on here? I asked your man Cal, but he said I'd better talk to you. He told me a few things, of course, about how a gang was trying to get the valley away

166

from old Alex Jenkins; at the same time, apparently, Jenkins has no legal right to it."

"That's about the size of things, Sam. I'll tell you briefly about what has happened. . . ."

Blaine listened intently while Johnny outlined the situation. When Johnny had finished he frowned. "Offhand, I'd say there wasn't much chance of dislodging those farmers," Blaine said. "I don't just understand about those leases, though."

"That's got me wondering too. Cassidy is working some sort of crooked plan, but I just can't put my finger on it. A man like Cassidy doesn't suddenly start working to help a bunch of farmers just for the fun of it."

"Has Cassidy himself taken out a lease?"

"No, so far as I know."

At that moment Cal Henry mounted to the porch. Johnny said, "Cal, take these two empty beer bottles back and bring out three full ones, will you?" When Cal had disappeared inside the Cash Deal, Johnny turned back to Blaine. "When we finish our drinks, Sam, you'd better head down to the hotel and get yourself a room."

"I won't bother with getting a room. There's quite a bit of daylight left, and my crew should be showing up shortly. When it does we'll get started pronto. I realize you're in a hurry to get this job done and every minute counts. I've been looking over maps and I figure we'll strike out for the Rio Pinto and then just follow it up to its head. It runs an almost due-north course straight up the valley."

Johnny nodded. "The Cross-J ranch house is located on the west side of the river, about five or six miles south of its head. I don't know whether to tell you to stop off and visit Alex Jenkins or not. I reckon not; he's feeling right sore these days."

Cal returned with the beer, and the men sipped the foamy amber liquid in silence for the next few minutes. Blaine finally put down his bottle with a long sigh. "That's right good on a hot day, Johnny."

Cal chuckled. "Does the day have to be hot so you can enjoy beer?"

Blaine smiled and turned back to Johnny. "Where'll I find you if it becomes necessary to see you in a hurry? Something might come up; a man never knows."

"I'll be around town here — maybe at the hotel or the sheriff's office — or out to the Cross-J. If you're near the Cross-J it might be wise to stop there first."

"Well, I'll be getting started just as soon as my men arrive —"

"Rider coming!" Cal announced.

The three men gazed down the street, where a horse could be seen approaching rapidly. Cal said after a minute, "It looks like Brazos Burnett."

When he stopped before the saloon the rider proved to be Burnett. He pulled his pony up short in a scattering of dust and gravel, tossed reins over the hitch rack, and strode angrily up on the porch, his features crimson with rage.

Johnny commenced, "Howdy, Brazos. What brings you — ?"

"Thought I might find you here," Brazos snarled. "Now you got Alex hawg-tied, you just set around taking your ease and letting things go plumb to hell —"

"Wait a minute, wait a minute," Johnny interposed. "What's got you all upset? Oh yes, Brazos Burnett, this is Sam Blaine. He's here to survey the valley and —"

Brazos nodded shortly to Blaine. "Another buzzard come to the feast, I reckon."

"Now, look here, Burnett," Blaine began testily. "I don't know what you mean and —"

"Get down to cases, Brazos," Johnny insisted firmly. "You can't go around calling names without you give a good reason. We want an explanation, man."

"You'll get it," Burnett snapped. "Auburn, you've certainly played hell with the Cross-J. It was a sorry day when you rode into this range."

"I'll concede that, if it will make you feel any better," Johnny said quietly. "But I'm asking that you tell me what's wrong."

"As if you didn't know," Burnett said hotly.

"I'm asking," from Johnny.

"I suppose it ain't your doings," Burnett rasped. "It was probably you told those farmers to fence off the Cross-J —"

"Just a minute," Johnny said swiftly. "I gave no permission to anybody to fence off the Cross-J. Who are the farmers? How many are there?"

"Thirty-five or forty, led by a plug-ugly named Rufe Howard. Ben Cassidy's out there too. Cripes a'mighty! We could have cleaned the scuts out, only Alex won't let us make a move. Alex says he passed his word to you; he give us orders not to interfere. You still insisting you don't know about it?"

"I sure am," Johnny said.

"We-ell" — Burnett looked uncertain — "maybe you can do something about it, then Alex won't make a move to stop it, and he won't let the hands do anything either. Pat, she tells me to ride and find you." His rage suddenly got the better of him. "Dammit to hell! Those farmers are just like a lot of buzzards now that you've got Alex stopped. He just sets there, sort of helpless — with all those buzzards gathered around to pick his bones like he was a dying buffalo bull. All right, Auburn, what you going to do about it? They're running fence clean around the buildings, cutting us off complete — and Cassidy sitting his horse, laughing fit to kill, boasting that the Ranger gave the farmers the go-ahead. So help me, Auburn, I'd like to throw a slug of lead through your interfering guts —"

"All right." Johnny nodded. "I reckon I know how you feel. Maybe I'll give you the chance, Burnett, but not right now. Right now you'd better save that lead. You may need it." He spun around to Cal Henry. "Cal, you slip back to the livery. Get your horse and saddle up Cherokee for me."

"What you aiming to do?" Burnett asked.

"We're going to stop those blasted, billy-be-damned farmers," Johnny snapped. "I never gave permission for anything like this. So save your lead, Burnett, save your lead. You may be burning powder presently!"

Cal left for the livery stable at a run. Brazos gulped. He didn't say anything for a moment or two. Finally he blurted, "Look, Johnny, mebbe I run off at the head more'n I should. It just made me so damned mad —"

"Forget it," Johnny said shortly. "I'm commencing to get mad myself. Meanwhile, Brazos, while we're waiting for Cal, slip inside and drink a beer. We got a hot, dusty ride ahead." He turned to Sam Blaine. "You'll get started just as soon as your men and wagon arrive, won't you?"

"I already told you that," Blaine said.

Johnny nodded. "I know you did, but you didn't realize when you made that statement just what sort of farmers there are in this country. They're mad-dog mean."

Blaine smiled. "My men carry guns as well as surveying equipment, Johnny. We don't scare easily. You go ahead with your job; you can count on me to do mine."

Johnny said thanks gratefully. He glanced along the street and saw Cal approaching with the horses. By the time Cal arrived Brazos had emerged from the saloon, wiping his mouth with the back of his hand. Johnny said, "Come on, Brazos, we'll do some buzzard scattering, if possible. Sam, I'll see you later when we get things settled around." He started down to meet Cal, followed by Brazos.

Blaine called after them: "Well, boys, singe a few buzzard feathers for me."

Johnny laughed grimly as the three men climbed into saddles. "Singe, hell!" he snapped. "I figure before we get through we'll have a complete skinning job on our hands!"

XVI. Gun-whipped

The sun was edging near the tops of the cedar-crested hills by the time Johnny, accompanied by Cal and Brazos, drew near the Cross-J. As they neared the last bend in the well-worn trail, before coming in sight of the ranch buildings, their ears caught the far-off sounds of revelry; there were some drunken singing, loud voices, considerable laughter, and some cursing. A few minutes later, as the riders circled a stand of post-oak trees, they came upon a scene that made the blood course angrily through their veins.

On the long front gallery of the ranch house were several individuals in overalls, lounging in various attitudes of repose. There were wagons scattered about, rolls of wire and piles of still-unused posts. There were a number of idly grazing horses. A small keg of whisky stood on one wagon; most of the men were gathered at that point. Near by, two men sat laughing in saddles, tin cups of whisky in their hands. One of the men was Ben Cassidy; the other, a burly, beetle-browed individual in new overalls, wearing a holstered forty-five, Johnny didn't know.

"The dirty coyotes," Brazos grated. "They're making a celebration of this."

Shiny new wire stretched all around the ranch buildings as far as they could see. The Cross-J was completely hemmed in. Of the Cross-J crew, not a man was in sight.

Johnny said, "Who's the big bruiser with Cassidy?"

Cal replied, "I've seen him in town but don't know his name."

"Name's Rufe Howard," Brazos growled. "He's sort of a leader of the farmers — next to Cassidy — and a lousy varmit if there ever was one —" He pulled up short. "What the hell!"

"Dammit!" Johnny exclaimed. "The fools have fenced straight across the roadway."

"That fence wa'n't up when I left," Brazos said.

"It's not going to be up much longer, either," Johnny snapped.

Barring their path with new posts on either side of the roadway, was a four-strand, brand-new wire fence. There wasn't any gate in it.

Johnny said, "Either of you hombres carry a pair of wire cutters?"

"Ain't got mine with me — dammit!" Cal said.

Brazos drew his cutters out of a hip pocket. "Mine ain't ever been away from me since this fence-stringing started," he said angrily, starting to get down from his saddle.

"It's your job, Brazos," Johnny said.

Brazos didn't require any urging. He cut savagely at the wire which twanged viciously as it whipped free from its tautly strung bondage. Four times, Brazos manipulated his wire cutters, and when he had finished the roadway was open to travel again. Brazos climbed back in his saddle, grunting, "That's one job I sure enjoyed, but it looks like I'm going to exchange my cutters for a six-gun right now."

Rufe Howard and Ben Cassidy had witnessed the fence-cutting and were tearing toward them, quirting their ponies, as Johnny and his two companions rode on through the opening in the fence.

Howard reached them first. He pulled his pony to a halt that jerked it to haunches. "What in hell do you think you're doin'?" he howled.

"We're not; it's done," Johnny said calmly.

Howard's right hand was already resting on the butt of his six-shooter. "I suppose you're that Ranger I been hearin' about. Goddammit! You gave us permission to fence — ain't that right, Ben?" as Cassidy rode up and nodded to Johnny.

"That's as I understood it," Cassidy said coldly. "You going back on your word, Auburn?"

"I never gave you permission to fence off a

public highway," Johnny said in chilly accent. "This roadway runs all the way from Painted Post, clear up to Dodge City. It's been in use for years. It can't be closed without permission of the county supervisors —"

"T'hell with all that!" Howard snarled. "We worked hard stringin' this fence. We ain't goin' to —"

"You're going to do what the law says," Johnny snapped. "Nobody but a fool would try to fence off a public thoroughfare."

"You callin' me a fool?" Howard flared.

"You and anybody else that ordered this wire-stringing!" Johnny's words cracked like rifleshots.

"Now look here, Auburn," Cassidy said. "We had your word that —"

"That I wouldn't interfere with the stringing of wire on your leases," Johnny interrupted. "Cripes, Cassidy! You should know better than to shut off a highway that's been open to public travel for years. Now if you want to be tough about it, that suits me right down to the ground. Trouble with you is you're so damned anxious to make things hard for Alex Jenkins, you haven't used good judgment. The fence is down where the road goes through, and, so help me, it's going to stay down!"

"That's the talk, Johnny." Cal grinned.

Brazos was looking at Johnny, wide-eyed with satisfaction. "By the A'mighty," he growled. "Maybe the Ranger is shooting straight."

"I figured that way almost from the first," Cal said.

Johnny wasn't listening to the two. He sat his saddle easily, facing the angry Cassidy and Howard. Both were groping for words to reply, but for the moment Johnny had them stopped.

Johnny laughed contemptuously after a moment. "Well, it's up to you two. Your fence is down. You figuring to leave this highway open, or would you like to call your men and start putting it up again? Either way suits me. As a matter of fact, I'd just a little sooner you'd decide to get tough about this business and try to put up the fence again. *Try*, I say. I'm getting almighty sick of putting up with the crooked business that goes on in this country, and I'm sure aching to burn powder. Is that clear, Cassidy — Howard?"

While they were talking other of the farmers had noticed them and left the whisky keg to draw near. Johnny could see they were all slightly tipsy and spoiling for trouble.

Howard was swearing steadily under his breath by this time, but he wasn't saying anything directly to Johnny. He seemed to be waiting to take his cue from Cassidy.

Cassidy started to speak, stopped. He swallowed heavily and forced a smile. "No use you getting proddy, Auburn," he said. "We aim to obey the law. Fact is, stringing that fence across the road was a mistake —"

"I knew that the minute I saw it," Johnny interrupted coldly. "I'm glad to hear you realize the fact — or maybe I'm not."

"You don't know what I mean," Cassidy continued. "We didn't notice there was a road there, and the boys got plumb enthusiastic about their work. First thing you know, we were all fenced in complete. We were laughing about it, me'n Rufe, just as you arrived. Ain't that right, Rufe?"

"Yeah, that's right," Howard said sullenly. One hand still gripped his gun butt, and Johnny was watching him narrowly.

More of the farmers had arrived now and were standing around, listening angrily. One of them yelled, "Don't you take nothing off'n that Ranger, boss."

Johnny wasn't sure whether he was calling to Howard or Cassidy. He turned to Cassidy. "Tell your rats to shut up," he snapped. "We got more business here."

The crowd surrounding the horses fell silent.

Cassidy said uneasily, "What other business you meaning?"

Johnny explained. "It looks to me as if you had the Cross-J buildings completely fenced in."

"That's right," Cassidy admitted. "Rufe is taking over this section of land. If Jenkins' buildings happen to be on the property, that's too bad. He'll have to get 'em off — or leave 'em for Rufe." There was considerable satisfaction in Cassidy's voice.

"I'm not so sure he will," Johnny said coldly. "I want to see the lease that gives Howard this particular section."

Cassidy looked uneasy, then said, "Show him the lease Rufe."

Howard produced a folded sheet of paper and reluctantly passed it over to Johnny. Johnny glanced at the written words and the signature at the bottom. The paper was signed with the name of Edward Santee, the land agent at Austin, Texas.

Johnny folded the paper and handed it back. "It don't work, Cassidy," he said. "That paper just calls for a section of leased land. It doesn't say any particular section."

"How in hell can it designate a particular section," Cassidy demanded, "when this valley hasn't even been surveyed yet? You told me that yourself. Howard's lease calls for a section of open land in Painted Post Valley, Painted Post County. This is the section he's taking."

Johnny shook his head. "No, he's not. So far as surveying goes, Sam Blaine, the surveyor, arrived today. He's already on his way up the valley. Once this section is surveyed, you and your nester friends can go about picking the sections they want — maybe. But the sections on which the Cross-J buildings stand aren't to be claimed. They're Alex Jenkins', until some court decides otherwise."

"By God!" Cassidy shouted angrily. "What right has Alex Jenkins got to the land and buildings?"

"Squatter's rights," Johnny snapped. "You'll find they stand up right well in court after a man has lived on a property a number of years."

A howl of rage left Rufe Howard's lips. "You meanin' to say I'm not goin' to get that house and —"

"That's exactly what I'm meaning!" Johnny flashed. "So you'd better get out of here pronto!"

Howard threw discretion to the wind and called Johnny a name. It was a name no white man will take without fighting.

For just a brief instant Johnny paused, his eyes steady on Howard's red-rimmed, hate-filled gaze. Howard's hand was again on that gun butt. Then Johnny moved with the speed of lightning; he spurred his horse in close. One hand went down to holster. His gun came up, swinging savagely, to land with crushing force against the side of Howard's head, before Howard's gun was clear of its holster. Howard swayed and started to fall from the saddle. Johnny hit him again as he went down. The man didn't even groan as he struck the earth.

Cassidy started to speak, but Johnny cut him short. "Get your men busy, Cassidy," Johnny said, "if you want to keep your wire. I'll give you time to yank up those posts and reroll the wire, if you like. Or you can all get off Cross-J property now. Suit yourself, but you've got to think fast. My patience is just about at an end. One way or the other, you've got to get out — clear off Cross-J property proper —"

"By God, we won't!" Cassidy stormed. "How about it, men? You going to be run off by this Ranger after all your hard work?"

"No!" "Not by a damn sight!" "We're stayin'!" and similar yells were heard. Johnny caught the flashing of several guns. A triumphant smile crossed Cassidy's face. Johnny, Cal, and Brazos moved their horses back a trifle, preparing to reach for guns.

And then came a sudden interruption as wild yells were heard and the Cross-J crew came pouring around the corner of the house, with Yank Ferguson in the lead.

"We're coming, Johnny!" Yank yelled. "We knew you didn't want us to hold in any longer when you gun-whupped that Howard skunk. We start throwin' lead when you say the word!"

The men back of Cassidy looked somewhat startled at the interruption, then quickly regained their confidence. After all, they outnumbered the Cross-J men. But apparently

Ben Cassidy took a different view of the situation. He held up one hand for silence. His voice shook with anger when he spoke. "All right, Auburn, we'll get out. We'll take our wire and posts first, though. We'll get out for now. But you haven't heard the last of this. Only that you're a Ranger and got the law on your side, it wouldn't be settled this easy. But I aim to obey the law. We'll get out."

Johnny nodded, cold-eyed. "Keep your men working until every strand of wire and every post is away, Cassidy. Something else, if you do any fencing anyplace else, don't take any Cross-J cows. It'd be wisest to drive 'em out first."

Cassidy's face was purple with anger. His right hand kept straying down toward his holster. "Damn you!" he grated. "If you wasn't a Ranger —"

Johnny laughed contemptuously. "Come on, cowboys," he said, "let's go talk to Alex Jenkins and tell him the law works both ways sometimes, even if it isn't always a good law."

They started back toward the ranch house, Brazos riding at Johnny's side. There was a catch in his voice when he said, "Johnny, I'd sort of like to apologize to you."

Johnny smiled warmly. "Forget it, Brazos," he said. "Just consider me as one of the Cross-J from now on. That's all I'm asking."

XVII. Ranger Courage

It was about ten that night. Johnny Auburn and Sheriff Obie Grant sat on the porch in front of the sheriff's office, smoking cigarettes. Out in front, at the hitch rack, Johnny's pony stood, the sweat on its flanks drying in the soft breeze that swept down Chisholm Street from the sage-dotted range beyond the town. Overhead the stars were as big as tin cups and just as shiny in the indigo sky.

Obie's cigarette butt described a glowing arc as he shot it out to the roadway and commenced manufacturing another cigarette. Along the street on either side lights from the saloons made yellow rectangles in the dust. Occasionally a pair of high heels clumped along the board sidewalks. Otherwise the town was quiet.

Obie stirred when Johnny had finished talking. "By cripes! Johnny, you sure handled the situation plumb elegant. I imagine old Alex feels a heap different about you now."

"Some," Johnny admitted. "It did me good to see his eyes brighten up again. He was sure sunk for a spell. It's good, knowing the

183

crew feels different too. I hated to see Cal Henry leave the Cross-J because of me. He belongs there; this time I hope to see him stay."

Obie said dryly, "Of course it didn't make any difference to Pat either."

Johnny's cheeks flushed in the darkness. "I reckon Pat and I are getting to understand each other," he conceded.

"I reckon," Obie chuckled. He added, after a moment, "And Cassidy and his gang really got off the Cross-J tonight, eh?"

Johnny answered in the affirmative. "That gang sure worked under the lash of Cassidy's cursing. He even made Rufe Howard pitch in after Howard recovered consciousness. They got every bit of wire and every post loaded before I left. Then I rode in to tell you. They're clear of the Cross-J — for the present, anyway."

"You expecting more trouble?"

"Gosh yes. We're just getting nicely into it now. Y'know, Obie, those men of Cassidy's call themselves farmers, but they're the queerest-looking farmers I ever saw. They look like they'd all bought their overalls about the same time; they all carry six-shooters. Most of 'em got bronc-warped legs, too."

"Probably a bunch of no-good punchers and rustlers that just thrun in with Cassidy for a big land grab," Obie speculated.

"That's about the way I size up matters. Oh, say, did Sam Blaine's crew arrive?"

Obie said they did and added, "Sam didn't lose any time getting them started on the job. They left town before sundown."

"That's good." Johnny hesitated a moment, then said uncomfortably, "Obie, life is going to grow increasingly difficult for you from now on."

Obie didn't reply for a moment; then, "I don't get you."

Johnny explained: "Henceforth, all the law-enforcing is going to be on your shoulders. It's up to you to keep things peaceful in this neck of the range — if possible. And I'm afraid it's going to be pretty damn impossible."

"I still don't get you." In the darkness Johnny had to guess at the puzzled frown on Obie's face. "You're not figuring to pull out, are you?"

"I'm staying."

"You're a Texas Ranger. That's good enough law to suit me, Johnny."

"But I'm not, Obie. I resigned from the Rangers a few days back. Headquarters has my letter by now."

A sort of choking sound escaped Obie; then there was a long silence. Finally he said in a weak voice,

"Bu-but what's the idea?"

Johnny said, "I was sent here to do a job

of law-enforcing. I did it. But I didn't like the job. For once, it seems, the law worked for the wrong side. Obie, I quit the Rangers so I could throw in with Alex Jenkins. We're going to get rid of Cassidy or die a-trying."

"Oh, geez!" Obie groaned. "Just when I thought everything was settled and we'd have no more range war. Cripes, Johnny! Things will get worse than ever now, Geez! The way it looks to me, you've turned completely around and rebelled against everything the Rangers stand for."

"For the moment I reckon I have," Johnny admitted moodily.

"I might be even forced to arrest you," Obie said suddenly.

"It's possible."

"This," Obie said angrily, "is a hell of a note." He puffed irately on his cigarette, and the resulting glow brought out the disturbed lines on his features. "Does Cassidy know you're not a Ranger any more?"

"No. I told the folks out to the Cross-J."

Obie gave a long sigh of relief. "Don't tell Cassidy. You can run a bluff on him any time you like, and he won't dare buck you, because he'll figure he'd be bucking Ranger law."

"It won't work, Obie. I had something of the sort in mind for a spell, but I feel crooked as hell posing as something I'm not. I've thrown in with the Cross-J, and we're going to do what we've set out to do as square and peaceful as we know how. That means that Cassidy has to know I've resigned."

"I don't like the setup," Obie stated bluntly. "I saw Cassidy and Rufe Howard ride in just a few minutes before you arrived. They went down to the Maverick Saloon. Cold-Deck is down there. And Tascosa Jake Wiley — and Gawd only knows how many more of Cassidy's thugs. What do you think would happen to you if they knew you weren't a Ranger any more?"

"That's why I came in tonight — to tell Cassidy."

Stunned silence on Obie's part, then the outburst, "Why, you crazy idjit! Johnny, they'd tear you limb from limb. I couldn't save you. They'd jump you when I wasn't around."

"Nevertheless," Johnny said stubbornly, "I'm going to tell Cassidy — tonight. I've got to take any risks that crop up. You see, this afternoon Cassidy kept saying that if only I wasn't a Ranger I couldn't get away with what I was doing. That's sort of stuck in my crop. Maybe I did take advantage of him. He deserves a square deal from me."

"Why in the name of the seven bald steers does he?" Obie asked hotly.

"Because I like to do business that way," Johnny said. He rose to his feet. "I'm going to drift down to the Maverick now and tell Cassidy that thought of the Rangers doesn't need to influence his feelings toward me."

"For Gawd's sake, don't!"

Johnny laughed softly. "Cassidy doesn't throw any scare into me."

"Not Cassidy alone. It's his whole gang. They'll jump you and —"

"My mind's made up, Obie."

"You stubborn fool! You've left the Rangers, but you sure got your Ranger courage left. All right, if you're determined to have trouble I'll go along with you just to see that there's fair play."

"I'd rather go alone, Obie. You see, there wasn't any peace officer present when I rode roughshod over Cassidy this afternoon. I figure I can take care of myself."

They argued for some time. Finally Obie reluctantly gave in. Johnny said, *Adiós,* and strode off in the direction of the Maverick Saloon. Obie gazed after him with dark forebodings until he'd gone out of sight and then rose and headed in the same direction.

After leaving Obie, Johnny stopped in at his hotel. From his valise he procured an extra belt and six-shooter which he strapped about his hips. Then he once more stepped to the street and walked slowly and deliberately toward the Maverick Saloon.

There was a great deal of loud talking in angry voices as Johnny stepped inside. They didn't notice him at once. Cold-Deck Malotte, Cassidy, Rufe Howard, and Tascosa were at the bar. There was quite a crowd of the farmers — so-called — there too. Johnny guessed that they were still very angry over the afternoon doings. Suddenly Cassidy glanced around, his gaze falling on Johnny as he approached the bar. Instantly Cassidy's face clouded up like a thunderstorm. He spoke swiftly to his companions. They, too, faced about, as did others in the room. Johnny could almost feel the concentrated hate that was directed at him. He was quick to notice several hands straying involuntarily toward holstered guns.

Cassidy said in a rasping voice, "You want to see me, Auburn?"

Johnny nodded. "You guessed it, Cassidy. This afternoon you voiced certain threats of what you'd do if I wasn't a Ranger. I resigned from the Rangers several days back. Now it's up to you, Ben Cassidy. Make your play! I'm waiting."

He stood there, cool thumbs hooked into cartridge belts, eyes steady on Cassidy's face as he noticed the man's features light up in almost fiendish joy. A low growl of hate rolled through the barroom.

"I'm waiting, Cassidy." Johnny's cold tones again cut through the room. "There's no Ranger authority to hold you back now. I've dealt the cards to your liking. It's your play!"

XVIII. Roaring Forty-fives

"It's what we've been waiting for, boss!" Tascosa Jake's voice was low, triumphant. He commenced to back a step, falling into a half crouch as he moved. At the same time Cassidy took one backward step. Cold-Deck Malotte and Rufe Howard started to spread out at the same instant.

But already a puzzled look was creeping into Cassidy's face. He put out one protesting hand in Tascosa's direction and spoke two words, "No, wait!"

By this time Johnny had backed to the bar and stood, elbows resting on the edge of the long counter, one boot heel hooked over the rail. His eyes shifted swiftly from man to man as he kept each gun under observation. Back of the bar, Louie, the bartender, approached stealthily, one clenched fist gripping a bung starter.

Johnny caught the sound of that stealthy step and sensed, rather than knew, what was taking place. He spoke coldly, without turning his head. "You, barkeep, keep away from in back of me. Get a gun and come round front if you want a hand in this game." Then as Louie hesitated uncertainly, "You hear me, you low-life rat? Get down to the end of the bar before I plug you!"

"You can't talk to my bartender like that —" Cold-Deck Malotte commenced.

"I am talking to him — just like that," Johnny said flatly. "You'd better keep your trap shut, Malotte. I'm waiting to hear from your boss." He smiled icily. "That is, if Cassidy hasn't lost his tongue. Speak up, Ben! I've arranged matters to your liking. What you aiming to do about it?"

The room had gone deathly still now as it waited for Cassidy to speak. Cassidy just stood there, eying Johnny as though he couldn't believe the import of the words Johnny had spoken.

"I don't get it," he said querulously. "What's the game, Auburn, you saying you've left the Rangers?"

"It's no game," Johnny replied promptly. "I'm stating truth. I came up here to enforce the law. I did it. I've explained honestly to you certain aspects of that law as it pertains to fencing off highways and jumping other men's claims. But where it pertains to Alex Jenkins I don't like that law. From now on out I'm for Jenkins. I'm sick of your kind using the law to get rich. I've quit the Rangers, Cassidy, so I can buck you and your kind from start to finish — and I intend to remain within the law doing it. Obie

Grant is the only law in this town now — that and the law laid down by old Sam Colt. Which kind do you want, Cassidy?"

"You've quit the Rangers," Cassidy said unbelievingly.

"Cripes! How many times do I have to tell you?" Johnny said impatiently. "You made certain threats of what you'd do if I wasn't a Ranger. All right, I'm not a Ranger any more. Have you got the nerve to carry out your threats, Cassidy?"

Cassidy said hoarsely, "I don't believe it, Auburn. This is a trick! Cold-Deck, Tascosa — don't let this hombre talk you into something. He's just looking for an excuse to bring all his Ranger pals into this valley. Keep your hands away from those guns."

Johnny laughed scornfully. "You're yellow, Cassidy."

Cassidy's face reddened. "No, I'm just smart," he growled. "You're not working me into any trap that will bring more Rangers here. Me, I obey the law. The same goes for my friends."

"You're yellow clear through," Johnny repeated. "You were yellow when you shot that boy over in Santa Angela a few years back. I don't mind telling you, Cassidy, I've been honing for your hide ever since then."

"By God!" Cassidy burst out. "I believe you came here looking for trouble."

Johnny smiled icily. "That fact just penetrated your thick skull, didn't it? Sure I came here looking for trouble. How about the threats you made this afternoon, Cassidy? Lost your nerve, have you?"

"I'll get you," Cassidy snarled. "But the time isn't now. I'm staying within the law until I learn what your game is. I ain't a fool, Auburn —"

"I'm commencin' to think you are," Rufe Howard blurted hotly. "Ben, you goin' to take this off'n Auburn — after what he done this afternoon?"

"You, Rufe" — Cassidy spoke swiftly — "keep your mouth shut."

"T'hell I will!" Howard spat savagely. "This is our best chance. I'm takin' it. Jerk your iron, Auburn!"

He'd already started to draw his gun when he first commenced speaking. It was halfway from holster when he challenged Johnny to draw.

Johnny laughed with grim satisfaction, threw himself to one side as Howard's first shot ripped into the front of the bar. He was moving too fast to make a good target as his hands darted to holsters. Two slugs struck the floor as the twin guns flashed up to bear on Howard. Heavy reverberations rolled through the barroom. Crimson gunfire flared dully in the powder smoke.

Howard coughed, swayed a moment. He took one uncertain step, then pitched face down on the pine planks, the six-shooter clattering from his hand to go sliding across the floor.

Through the drifting wave of smoke Johnny's voice came cool and challenging and steady as he backed toward the door. "Up with 'em, you scuts! Who's next? If you don't want me to raise 'em high, you'd better reach fast. Come on, draw somebody!"

He stood there, poised on the balls of his feet, the leveled six-shooters, moving just enough to cover the whole roomful of men. Several arms were already in the air.

"Think you're tough, eh?" Johnny taunted. "I aim to show some of you would-be badmen what tough really means. What's the matter, have you all gone yellow? Hasn't anyone guts enough to draw?"

All hands were in the air now. There was something of awe in the eyes of the men facing Johnny.

"By God, Auburn!" Cassidy said hoarsely. "I believe you've gone crazy!"

Johnny's chill laughter cut through the room. "No, I'm just smart." He repeated Cassidy's words of a few minutes before. "I tried to give you hombres a break within the law, but you couldn't understand that. There's only one thing you do understand. That's gun talk! I aim to give you plenty of that and nothing more from now on out. Understand?"

Silence greeted his words. Most of the men had backed considerably farther from him by this time. Only Cassidy, Tascosa, and Cold-Deck retained their positions, their arms high in air.

Disgust suddenly entered Johnny's voice. "You three — put your hands down!"

Warily Cassidy and his two companions lowered their arms, watching Johnny's every move. Suddenly Johnny, moving swiftly, thrust both weapons back in holsters.

"Now," he said slowly as he hooked his thumbs in his belts, "have any of you three got the nerve to draw?"

Cassidy and Cold-Deck remained motionless. Only Tascosa's right arm moved a trifle; then he changed his mind.

"Go on, Tascosa, go through with it," Johnny said encouragingly. "Let's see you handle those two Colts of yours."

For just a brief instant Tascosa hesitated; then he gulped and shook his head, throwing both arms wide of his sides. "This ain't the time for it," he growled.

Johnny said, "Oh hell," in a weary tone. His left hand worked at the buckle of one belt. The next instant a belt and holstered gun slipped to the floor. "My one gun against yours, Tascosa," he pleaded. "Now will you take a chance with your two hawg-legs?"

Again Tascosa shook his head. "This ain't

the time for it," he repeated.

Johnny's sarcastic laughter cut through the room like a sharpened steel blade. "Cripes a'mighty!" he snorted contemptuously. "You're just a bunch of rabbits. All right, you've had your chance. From now on *I'm* the hard-boiled hombre on this range. Any one of you would-be gun-slingers that cuts my trail had better move plumb cautious, because I'm sure wearing war paint and I'm plenty proddy!"

The doors at his back swung open, and Obie Grant pushed in. "I reckon this has gone about far enough," Obie grunted. "Johnny, you pick up your belt and gun and keep them lead throwers both out of sight."

"Look here, Grant" — Cassidy suddenly found his voice — "I demand that you arrest Auburn for the murder of Rufe Howard. Auburn's no longer a Ranger. You've got the authority. Auburn came here and picked a fight with Howard, shot him down without a chance —"

"Cut it," Obie snapped. "I know how much chance he had. I watched the whole business over the top of the swinging doors. Howard drew first. Auburn fired in self-defense. There's no cause for arrest that I know of. Furthermore, I heard Johnny give you coyotes one of the sweetest dressing downs it's ever been my good fortune to hear. I think he acted like a damn fool, but I sure got to admire his nerve. Come on, Johnny, let's get out of here."

"I demand justice!" Cassidy raged.

"What do you want me to do — send for the soldiers, or another Ranger?" Obie asked sarcastically. "You'll get justice, all right, Cassidy, or I miss my guess. You came within an ace of getting justice tonight — only you lacked the guts to meet it."

By this time Johnny had retrieved his belt and gun. "I'm ready," he said quietly. "Let's go, Obie. It sure stinks in this place."

Together they passed out of the Maverick, with no further word of protest being offered by Cassidy.

Once more on the street, Obie heaved a long sigh of relief. Johnny smiled wryly when he heard the sound. "Just between you and me," he drawled, "I feel the same way."

"Johnny, you fool — you utter damned fool," Obie said in exasperated tones. "I wasn't far behind you. You sounded like you'd gone completely crazy. What in hell did you think you were doing?"

"Throwing a scare into those hombres," Johnny said soberly. "A good deal of what I did was pure acting. I wasn't near as mad as I sounded. There was a heap of bluff in the whole business."

"But why?"

"The more hombres I can throw fear into, the fewer guns I'll be called on to face. I don't like shooting and killing, Obie, but the sooner we can stop Cassidy and his gang, the less killing there's going to be. Do you see what I mean?"

"I dunno," Obie grunted. "All's I do know is that you displayed enough cold nerve for twenty Rangers. I just hope your idea works, is all."

"If it don't we'll really get tough." Johnny laughed.

Obie said sarcastically, "What were you doing back there — just playing house?"

"No, talking myself dry. Do you suppose the Cash Deal would have a couple of cold bottles handy?"

"The Cash Deal had better," Obie replied. "You sure earned one. I reckon I did too; my knees ain't stopped shaking yet!"

XIX. "We'll Make the Breaks!"

The following day, Johnny rode out to the Cross-J where he was due to be greeted with open arms by the whole crew. The news of his doings the previous night at the Maverick had spread all over town. Cal Henry had come in early for the mail and heard the story. He had at once hurried back to the ranch to tell the news and had arrived an hour or so before Johnny.

When Johnny rode in he saw Pat and her father sitting on the front gallery of the house. Alex's bull-like voice was raised in a cordial greeting: "Stop here and let me congratulate you, Johnny, before you put up that horse."

"On what?" Johnny asked, slipping down from the saddle and stepping up on the porch. He dropped into a chair next to Pat. "How's it going this morning?"

"How's it going to go after this morning?" Pat said seriously. "That's what I'm thinking of."

"She means," Alex boomed, "that we're all sort of worried what's going to happen to you after that play you made in the Maverick last night."

"Oh, that," Johnny said modestly. "I don't reckon it was much. I just got the jump on those sidewinders, and they lost their nerve momentarily. How'd you hear about it?"

"Cal Henry brought the news just a spell ago," Pat explained.

"That so?" from Johnny. "I didn't see Cal in town. He usually drops into the Cash Deal when he comes in for the mail."

Alex chuckled heavily. "Hell's bells! Cal could hardly wait to get back here and tell us about it. You're sure of a warm welcome at the bunkhouse when you go down, Johnny. I even heard Yank Ferguson say he'd like to run you for state senator. That's how popular you've become."

"Seems like," Johnny said dryly, "the boys have changed their ideas of me in the past day or so."

"Johnny, we all have," Alex said earnestly. "Your way was right, but I was just too blame stubborn to see it. I sort of lost my head for a spell, I reckon. But between you and Pat, I think I've found it again." His voice grew more serious. "I still don't see, though, how you expect to save the Cross-J for us. Legally, Cassidy and his crowd still have the right to grab off everything except the land this house stands on."

"All I ask," Johnny said, "is that you leave matters to me. We'll just have to play along for the breaks for a time before I can act —"

"And if the breaks don't come?" Alex asked.

"We'll make 'em, then," Johnny said determinedly. "By the way, Alex, I've got a surveyor going over this valley. Man named Sam Blaine. He's white. I wish you'd tell your hands to treat him that way if they should run across him someplace."

"I'll do that — but why a surveyor?"

"It'll be pretty tough getting a clear title until this valley has been surveyed. I meant to tell you about this last night, but I was in such a hurry to get to town that it slipped my mind. I must have figured that Cal would tell you."

"Cripes," Alex said, "we haven't been able to get much out of Cal about what happened when he was under your orders. He always says to ask you."

Johnny smiled. "He's still obeying instructions, I reckon. Maybe I'd better pay his salary instead of you from now on, Alex. Say, do you happen to know if this valley was ever surveyed before? That is, I know it was, but what do you know about it?"

"Nothing," Alex replied promptly. "Didn't know surveyors had ever come in here —" He paused suddenly. "Wait a minute. Maybe I did hear something like that one time. Now what was it?" A deep frown furrowed his forehead. "Yes, I do remember something about it; I'd plumb forgotten before. Cripes, that must be twenty years back — mebbe more. I know now. This house wasn't finished then. The rest of the buildings were just shacks. I had a herd to deliver to the soldiers up in Kansas Territory. The Comanches were right ornery about that time, and I was afraid to leave Pat and her mother behind, so they went on trail with me and my hands. There wasn't anybody left here. We'd hardly left when the Comanches came in and burned everything and run off the cows that were left. It must have been that year the valley was surveyed. I dimly remember hearing that it had been, but I was so wrought up over the Comanches that I didn't pay much attention. Never did get the right of it. A circuit preacher told me that he'd seen surveyors in here and talked to 'em. They were under the impression that the Indians had wiped out everybody and that the land was clear for the taking."

"Dad," Pat said, "you never mentioned this before."

"Never gave it a thought," Jenkins said. "Never heard anything more of it. I suppose I figured that circuit preacher had been mistaken, and it quick slipped my mind. Johnny, you say it was surveyed?"

"So I understand." Johnny nodded. "By Sam Houston's orders." He went on and gave the details as he had had them from Blaine. When he had finished Alex Jenkins looked thoughtful. "So this place nearly belonged to Jesse Chisholm, eh? I'll be damned! At that, I'd sooner he'd had it than see it fall into Cassidy's hands."

"It won't fall into Cassidy's hands," Johnny promised.

Alex sighed heavily. "I wish I felt as sure as you do," he said. "By the way, Johnny, Brazos and Pat and I were talking about you at breakfast. We'd like a heap for you to come here and live while this trouble is going on. All the boys would like it too."

Johnny reddened with pleasure. "That's sure enough white of you people. I'll be glad to accept, though I'll keep my room at the hotel too. I'll probably be in town a lot until this business gets straightened out. Meanwhile, I'll take advantage of your offer and start in by staying to dinner today, if you'll have me."

"We'll have you any time," Pat said.

"You mean that?" Johnny asked.

Pat blushed under his steady gaze. "I reckon we mean what we say, cowboy."

Alex Jenkins' brows lowered as he looked from the girl to Johnny; then a deep chuckle rumbled up from his chest. Now it was Johnny's turn to redden. To cover his confusion he said, "I note you're not carrying your arm in a sling this morning, Alex."

"Cripes a'mighty, no," Alex boomed. "I got so blame sick and tired of lugging my wing around in that hammock, like I was crippled, or something, that I just couldn't stand it any longer. It was all Doc Kilburn's fool idea anyway. My wound wa'n't much more than a scratch — and where would I be if I found call to use a Winchester in a hurry? Nope, that sling is out from now on."

Johnny laughed, rose to his feet. "I reckon I'll go put Cherokee in the corral. See you come dinnertime." He stepped out and climbed into the saddle.

Pat eyed the pony a moment. "Darn pretty horse," she commented. "Cal was telling about him. I understand Cherokee can cook and darn socks."

"Those are just a couple of his minor accomplishments," Johnny said gravely. "Lately I've been teaching him to cut wire."

"Think there's be much more to cut?" Alex asked.

Johnny shook his head. "I probably just wasted my time on the wire business. I've been thinking of sending him out to Sam Blaine to learn surveying, though." Johnny paused. "You see, when this trouble is over I might want to take up a few sections in these parts myself. Cherokee could save me a surveyor's fees."

"Now there is an idea." Pat laughed.

"You mean the saving surveyor's fees," Johnny asked innocently, "or taking up land hereabouts?"

"Both," Pat replied. "We like good neighbors, Johnny, and you seem to be proving up."

"Proving up, hell!" Alex said in his booming tones. "Johnny has already proved up — in no uncertain fashion."

"Dad," Pat protested, "do you have to swear?"

"Yes, daughter, I do," Alex replied seriously, "every so often. Swearing ain't so bad, but I'll be damned if I like profanity!"

Johnny laughed, doffed his sombrero, and reined Cherokee around the corner of the house in the direction of the bunkhouse, where a wild cowboy yell from Cal Henry greeted his arrival. Cal came through the bunkhouse doorway with a wide grin on his face. "Hello, you damn ol' fire-eater. I heard things about you in town this morning."

"You can't believe all you hear," Johnny said, reining in for a moment.

"If you've got my kind of ears you can," Cal said. "Here and now I state, without any further preambles or aforesaids, relative to the party of the first part, that you done yourself proud and plumb elegant, John Auburn, and that from now on henceforth if every man on the Cross-J will strive to his utmost to emulate your most laudable undertaking — and carrying through — the Ben Cassidy gang of low-down, gall-sored, spavined, two-bit skunks — up to and including the aforementioned Cassidy — will very shortly meet with their comeuppance."

"That" — Johnny smiled — "is quite a speech."

"It ain't so much," Cal said modestly. "I've been practicing on it ever since I heard what you did."

Brazos Burnett spoke admiringly from behind Cal: "As I get it, Johnny, you went sort of hawg-wild in the Maverick last night."

"Just proving once more," Yank Ferguson said bluntly, "how badly we misjudged you at first. My Stet hat is off to you, Ranger — I forgot, you're not a Ranger any more. It's sure tough on the Rangers to have to lose your kind of nerve."

Other men pushed out from the bunkhouse and made similar comments. Jiggs Monahan said, "Get out of that saddle, Johnny. I'll take Cherokee to the corral for you."

Johnny and the rest went into the bunkhouse. The men started making up cigarettes. Johnny glanced around and said, "Nobody seems to be out working today. What's the idea, Brazos?"

"Alex's orders," Brazos explained. "You see, we weren't sure but what Cassidy and his gang might try some more wire stringing today. Alex wanted us all on hand. There isn't so much to do right now, anyway. Our beef animals will take care of themselves, I reckon. Ordinarily we'd be riding the trail up to Dodge City this time of year, but the Cassidy bustard sort of jammed up proceedings."

"I don't suppose anything unusual happened last night after I left here," Johnny said.

"I was just coming to that," Brazos said. "Not that it's anything to be concerned about — probably didn't mean anything —"

"Get to it, Brazos." Johnny smiled.

"Well," Brazos went on, "one of Cassidy's farmers came here looking for you last night —"

"You mean he came gunning for me?" Johnny asked quickly.

Brazos shook his head. "No, the feller that came last night — shucks, it was about three o'clock this morning to be exact — wa'n't no gun slinger. Fact is, I got to admit he was quite a likable young feller; if he hadn't been running with Cassidy's outfit I'd probably have invited him to stay for breakfast. And he wasn't one of those plug-uglies like the rest of the farmers. This kid was a sure-enough sodbuster."

"But what did he want?"

Brazos shrugged his shoulders. "You got me. Wouldn't give his name. Just said he wanted to see you. He acted sort of scared, too, and kept glancing over his shoulder like mebbe he was being followed. I noticed him here yesterday when that wire stretching was

207

going on. He seemed to sort of hold back and not pitch in like the rest, as though he didn't like the job."

"Hmmm!" Johnny wondered. "Wish I knew what was on his mind. It would be a break for us if one of Cassidy's men would turn against him and tell us just what game Cassidy is playing here."

"Something else," Brazos remembered. "Shortly after he left I thought I heard a shot coming from down the trail a spell. I got out of my bunk again and went outside, but I couldn't hear anything more, unless — and I'm not sure of this — I might have heard the sounds made by two horses running fast. But the sound faded quick, so I couldn't be sure."

"Did this young farmer come on a horse?" Johnny wanted to know.

Brazos nodded. "But he was no rider. I could see that when he climbed back in the saddle. I tried to get him to tell me what he wanted to see you about, but he acted like he didn't trust anybody on the Cross-J — which is likely enough, I suppose, seeing he's a Cassidy man."

"I reckon," Johnny said absent-mindedly, wondering what it was all about.

"I'm surprised Alex didn't mention it to you," Brazos continued. "He thought he heard the shot, too, and yelled down to ask if I'd heard it. I guess he must have figured that I'd be best to tell you, seeing Alex didn't come outside."

Cal Henry said suddenly, "Johnny, I just heard Pat hailing you from the house."

Johnny got to his feet. "I guess dinner must be ready. I'll see you hombres later."

However, it was quite some hours later before Johnny again turned up at the bunkhouse. After dinner he sat on the gallery and talked to Pat and Alex until suppertime. After supper he sat on the gallery and talked to Pat. There was a nice moon too. Their conversation had very little to do with the current trouble, and Cassidy's name wasn't once mentioned.

Reluctantly Johnny rose to leave about nine o'clock. By this time the two were on extremely friendly terms.

"Do you have to go?" Pat asked, looking up at him through the darkness cast by the gallery roof. "The boys in the bunkhouse won't be turning in yet. Dad always goes to bed early, but —"

"I won't be staying the night," Johnny explained. "I keep thinking about that young farmer I told you about. I'd like to know what he wants to see me for."

Pat gave a mocking sigh. "You keep thinking about that farmer. And after all the nice things you've been saying I didn't think you were thinking about anybody but me."

Johnny grinned. "Error on my part. I

meant to say I suddenly remembered that young farmer. Shucks, girl! I don't want to go. I'd sooner stay. But maybe I can find the fellow in town."

"You crazy redhead" — Pat laughed a trifle nervously — "do you always have to be looking for trouble?"

"This might mean less trouble if I can find him."

Pat rose to her feet. "I reckon I've lost all my natural charm, when you go riding off to find a farmer and leave me here —"

And that was as far as she got, when Johnny's arms went around her and she found his lips seeking hers. For a brief moment she resisted, then gave in. After a minute she broke away, laughing a bit unsteadily. "That really doesn't mean a thing, you know," she said. "We're just friends —"

"It means you're my girl from now on," Johnny said boldly. "After all this trouble is settled I aim to show you what it really means."

"Pretty confident, aren't you, Mister Auburn?"

Johnny was suddenly humble. "As a matter of fact, I'm not, Pat." His manner abruptly changed to one of levity. "Don't detain me any longer, woman. I've got to drift. Hand me my hat from that chair and —"

"Say please." Pat smiled. "The way you talk to a gal, you'd think women were just made to wait on you."

"Not 'made,'" Johnny corrected; "'trained' is the word."

He reached for his hat, then seized her and kissed her again before she could protest. "It don't mean a thing," he told her lightly. "We're just friends, you know."

She broke away and backed toward the doorway. Johnny stepped down from the porch. "I'll be seeing you eventually — friend," he said.

Pat's voice came a bit shakily from the shadow of the doorway. "Oh, Johnny, take good care of my friend and don't run unnecessary risks. I'd really hate to lose my — friend." And then she was gone inside the house.

Johnny entered the bunkhouse whistling happily. Two or three of the men were stretched in bunks but not asleep. Brazos and Yank Ferguson were engaged in a game of cribbage. Cal Henry and the rest looked on or occupied themselves with old magazines.

Cal looked up when Johnny entered; then his eyes widened. "What happened to you? Did you stub your toe on a chunk of gold? I'll swear you look exactly like the *felis libyca domestica* that devoured, chewed up, digested, and was nourished upon the *serinus canarius* — or to you, my illiterate companion, the cat that ate the canary. What happened to you? You got stars in your eyes."

211

"And you got bats in your belfry." Johnny grinned. "If you don't quit studying that encyclopedia up to the house, Cal, you'll be talking beyond your mentality."

"My conversation," Cal said placidly, "is already beyond the mentality of the poor, uneducated laborers in this humble bunkhouse —"

A spurred boot whizzed past his ear to strike the wall beyond. Cal turned and grinned at Jiggs Monahan. "Jiggsy, if your aim with a six-shooter wasn't any better —" He broke off suddenly as he saw Johnny buckling on guns and belts. "Hey, where you going?"

"Painted Post," Johnny said. "I'm going to see if I can find that farmer kid around town."

"I'll go with you," Cal said, getting to his feet.

Johnny hesitated. "I'd like the company, but you're back on the Cross-J crew now. I don't know whether you're working with me or for Alex."

Brazos raised his head from the cribbage board to grunt, "Take the featherbrained idiot along with you, Johnny. He's only a pain in the neck around here. Besides, Alex gave orders he was to take instructions from you."

"Ah, at last I have proved my worth!" Cal exclaimed dramatically, hurrying to get his hat and gun.

"You've proved you're worse," Brazos contradicted.

"Worse than what?" Cal paused.

"There isn't anything worse," Yank Ferguson said insultingly. "Cal, you've sure struck bottom."

Cal grinned and hurried to join Johnny, who was already on his way to the corral.

"I'm afraid my type isn't appreciated around here," he sighed when they were saddling up.

Johnny put one booted foot against Cherokee's side and jerked tight his saddle cinch. He said gravely, "That's tough, Cal. You'll just have to make 'em appreciate the fineness of your soul through undeviating adherence to the goal that lies before you."

"Undeviating adherence," Cal murmured dreamily. "That's elegant. Fineness of my soul. I must remember to spring that on the boys. Fineness of my soul —"

"Or thickness of your head," Johnny chuckled. "Come on, you bird-brained ranny — let's ride!"

XX. Cassidy Builds an Alibi

Ben Cassidy, Cold-Deck Malotte, and Tascosa Jake Wiley lounged with their backs against the tie rail in front of the Maverick. Tascosa was fashioning a cigarette; Malotte and Cassidy smoked cigars. The full moon bathed the street with white light that intensified the darkness of the shadows between buildings. The three men had come outside, where they could converse without the danger of being overheard by the crowd in the barroom.

Cassidy laughed softly, gesturing toward the swinging doors of the saloon. "Auburn did you a good turn with his little act last night, Cold-Deck. I haven't seen your place so crowded since I came here. I'll bet the other saloons in town are losing business tonight."

Malotte grunted disgustedly. "I'd just as soon not have business if I have to get it that way. Cripes! Most of those hombres are inside just in hopes of seeing Auburn repeat that performance he staged last night. Me, if I never see Auburn again it will be too soon."

Tascosa cursed bitterly. "So help me, I'm going to plug that Ranger — or ex-Ranger, whatever he is — the first good chance I get."

"You'll never have a better chance than you had last night, Tascosa," Malotte said sarcastically. "There he was, inviting you to draw, and you lost your nerve."

"You were in on that invitation too," Tascosa said quickly.

Cold-Deck smiled superciliously. "I never claimed to be a rootin'-tootin' gun slinger like you. You should have shot him, Tascosa."

Tascosa shook his head. "Last night wasn't the right time. The cards were all running Auburn's way. Know what I mean? He was hot, see? No matter what he did, he couldn't lose. I've seen hombres like him in action before. When they're that hot they're right, see?"

"Not manufacturing an alibi, are you, Tascosa?" Cold-Deck smiled.

"Me? I don't need alibis —" Tascosa commenced.

"Tascosa is right, Cold-Deck," Cassidy put in. "Auburn had something last night. I just can't put my finger on it, and neither can any other man, but you get a fellow keyed up to just the right pitch, like Auburn was and he can't lose. Auburn was sharp, alert. He was equal to three or four men last night. It was once he couldn't fail, no matter what he

215

did. It was no time to buck him. I, for one, am glad I had sense enough to realize it."

"Sure," Tascosa said eagerly, "we only did what was smart. It's the dumb hombres like Rufe Howard who can't smell danger when it's stuck right under their nose. Don't worry, Cold-Deck, we'll get that Auburn yet, and we'll get him right."

"I hope it's soon, then," Cold-Deck said testily. "I've put quite a chunk of money into this plan, Ben, and I don't want to see it fall through. Wire costs money, not to mention horses and food and wages for all these phony farmers we're supporting. You shouldn't have been so anxious to get Jenkins' place, Ben."

"It'd all worked out right if it hadn't been for Auburn sticking his nose in," Cassidy growled.

"Wish I'd been there," Tascosa bragged. "Maybe Auburn wouldn't have got away with so much —"

"After last night," Cassidy said coldly, "I wouldn't talk was I you, Tascosa. You say he was hot last night. Well, he wasn't cool yesterday, either. And he had the advantage of me thinking he was a Ranger too. Ranger word is law, you know. I still don't know what to think about him. I can't see why he should quit the Rangers. Maybe he was just bluffing. But why?"

"Quit worrying about whether he was bluffing or not," Tascosa said harshly, "and lay plans to rub him out as soon as possible. That way it won't make any difference what *his* game is."

"Let's forget Auburn for the time being —" Malotte suggested.

"As if we could," came Tascosa's growled interruption.

"— and try to figure out where that damn Vincent is," Malotte finished.

Tascosa swore. "Trouble with Vincent, he was a real farmer. Dammit! Ben, I don't know what you ever took him in with us for."

"Three hundred dollars," Cassidy said dryly. "I talked to him like a Dutch uncle, trying to convince him that my land-development scheme had all the farmers in it it could handle. But somehow, when he kept insisting that I take his three hundred and get him a section — well, I just couldn't talk any longer."

"I got so blasted sick of hearing him tell how he wanted to get settled so he could have his wife come here," Malotte sneered, "that I damn nigh plugged him myself."

"I'd still like to know why he went to the Cross-J last night," Cassidy mused. "I told Nick to keep a sharp eye on his movements, but he got away from Nick when Nick's back was turned. Just grabbed one of the horses and beat it. After he left the Cross-J Nick threw down on him —"

"Nick ain't a bad shot," Tascosa cut in. "Maybe he scored a hit."

"Not enough to finish Vincent, anyway," Cassidy growled. "He was seen in town today. I've got a hunch he's still here, hiding out someplace. Money or no money, I can see now I should never have taken him in with us. He's been sort of suspicious of us right from the first. If we could only locate the bustard we could finish him off and feel easier in our minds. If he ever gets to blabbing to Auburn —"

"Aw, he doesn't know anything, anyway," Malotte put in. "What could Vincent tell Auburn?"

"Enough, maybe, to arouse his suspicions too."

Loud laughter from Tascosa broke in the words. "If Auburn's suspicions aren't already aroused I don't know what you call it."

"Maybe you're right, at that," Cassidy conceded somewhat sheepishly.

Running footsteps sounded along the street. The three men at the hitch rack turned to glance across the way. The runner came sprinting along Chisholm Street and turned left on Colorado Street. In a few moments he had passed out of sight.

"Somebody running to get Doc Kilburn, I'll bet," Cassidy speculated.

"What makes you think so?" from Malotte.

"It's late," Cassidy replied. "There's no

shooting. What other reason would a hombre have for running this time of night? Just to clinch the idea, Doc Kilburn lives on the corner of Colorado and Comanche streets."

"Reckon you're right," Malotte agreed. "Probably some faithful husband due to become a father, and Doc is needed to bring the little bundle of joy into this peaceful world."

"Bundle of squawk, you mean," Cassidy grunted.

"I don't know about that," Tascosa said thoughtfully.

"Don't tell me you've become an infant lover," Cassidy said sarcastically.

Tascosa said impatiently, "Don't talk like a fool, Ben. I mean that hombre didn't look like any expectant father to me. If I ain't sad mistaken that was Cal Henry from the Cross-J."

"So what if it was?" Cassidy said. "If somebody's sick on the Cross-J should we start fretting?"

"If Cal had come from the Cross-J," Tascosa pointed out, "he'd have stayed on his horse until he got to the Doc's. Cal was in town when it happened — whatever it was happened. Who was with him — Auburn?"

"We haven't heard any shooting," Malotte said.

"Maybe Auburn's been took with some bad sickness," Tascosa said hopefully.

Cassidy held up one hand for silence.

Footsteps could be heard clumping along the plank walk on the Maverick side of the street.

"More customers for my bar, I suppose," Malotte said.

The three men peered down the thoroughfare and made out a trio of dark figures approaching rapidly. Cassidy announced after a moment, "It's Nick. Dan and Andy are with him."

The next instant three of Cassidy's farmers stopped at the hitch rack. Cassidy said impatiently, "Well?"

"We've located him," replied the man named Nick. He was an ugly-visaged fellow, as were his two companions.

"You've found Vincent?" Malotte asked eagerly.

Nick nodded. "Auburn and Henry rode in a spell back. Vincent met them at Obie Grant's office. I think I must have hit Vincent last night. He moves sort of weak-like."

"We just saw Cal Henry heading over toward Doc Kilburn's," Tascosa said.

"Where's Vincent now?" Cassidy snapped. "Still at Grant's office?"

Nick shook his head. "Cal and Auburn took him over to the hotel. Probably to Auburn's room. It's at the back. You can see right in the window from the alley."

Nick fell silent. Cassidy drew hard on his cigar, studied its glowing tip a few minutes, then tossed it to one side. "Cold-Deck — Tascosa," he said. "Let's get a drink. I'm thirsty."

He started toward the saloon entrance, followed by Malotte.

Nick said, "No further orders, boss?"

Cassidy paused at the entrance. "You've already had your orders, Nick. We can't risk having Vincent alive in Painted Post. You three understand that. Do you think I want to be where I can't have an alibi when the blowoff comes? I'm going inside. Get going, boys, and make the job good."

The three nodded and started off down the street. Tascosa said, "Wait, I'll go with you." He turned to explain to Cassidy, "Auburn's in that same room. No use passing up a chance like this."

Cassidy's teeth gleamed whitely in the moonlight. "That's the best idea you've had in a long spell, Tascosa. I like it fine. Just don't make any slips."

"Not me," Tascosa bragged. He turned and hurried after Nick and his two companions. Cold-Deck and Cassidy watched them fade into darkness down the street, then turned and entered the barroom.

XXI. The First Clue

By riding hard Johnny and Cal had arrived at Obie Grant's hitch rack shortly before eleven o'clock. Obie had already turned in between blankets, and after dismounting Johnny and Cal were forced to pound on the office door to arouse him.

The door opened, and Obie appeared drowsily at the entrance, his long, skinny shanks looking grotesque beneath the hem of his nightshirt. Obie rubbed his eyes sleepily and grumbled, "Less noise, you hombres. You aiming to wake up the prisoners in my jail? Oh, it's you, Johnny — and Cal. Come on in. What's up?"

They followed him into the office, where he sat down on the rumpled blankets of his cot set against one wall, and drew on pants and boots. Then he rose and fumbled at the oil lamp on his desk. The wick sprang into flame. Obie blinked in the sudden light and commenced to fashion a cigarette.

"Sorry we had to pull you out of bed, Obie," Johnny apologized, "but something has come up, and I'd like to see if you know anything about it."

"Don't mention it." Obie yawned widely. "I'd had to get up in the morning, anyway." He drew deeply on his cigarette and brightened somewhat. "What's on your mind?"

Johnny glanced at the door in the back of the room which led to the jail cells. "You said something about prisoners back there. Any chance of them hearing us?"

Obie shook his head. "Just a couple of hombres sleeping off a drunk. Pair of punchers from the 33-Bar. They came in this afternoon and lifted a few. Somebody told 'em how you put the bee on the gang in the Maverick last night. It made 'em feel so good, they decided to really celebrate and started mixing their drinks. The dang fools had to sample every drink Urban had in the Cash Deal. 'Bout the time I came in they'd reached a bottle of purple stuff called cream of violets, or some such name. I knew the situation was getting desperate, then, and sure enough it was. You know what them blame fools were aiming to do?"

"What?" Cal grinned.

"They were fixing to head down to the Maverick and see could they pull the same stunt Johnny pulled last night. I knew they'd just get shot up, so I arrested 'em for their own protection. Only that Urban is mayor of Painted Post, I'd have arrested him too. He should know better than to carry all these strange foreign liquors. He don't seem to realize those things make people drunk. It ain't like wholesome beer and whisky. But Urban has had those colored drinks for a long time; some smart salesman foisted 'em upon him 'bout ten years back. I reckon he figured this was a good time to unload — Cripes, Johnny! I'm running off at the head and you came to talk business."

Johnny said, "Obie, one of Cassidy's farmers came out to the Cross-J looking for me last night — early this morning, rather. I've a hunch he might have something important to say. Brazos told him I'd come to town. I'm wondering if you've heard of anyone like that inquiring for me."

"Yes sir," Obie said unexpectedly, "I have. He's a slim, young sort of gaffer and looks like a real farmer. Name's Jabez Vincent. He looked pale, like he was sick, or something."

"Did he come here asking for me?" Johnny asked.

Obie nodded. "He was here twice today. I told him you'd left for the Cross-J and that he could probably find you there. He looked worried as hell and said he didn't want to leave town. I asked why, and he wouldn't say. Wouldn't say what he wanted to see you about, either. I thought maybe it was a plan to bump you off, or something, but he didn't have a gun and he looked harmless. Still, he's one of the Cassidy crowd, so I don't know."

"You don't know where he is now?"

Obie shook his head. "He came the last time just before supper. Wanted to know if I could tell him when you'd be back. I couldn't, of course. I told him again to ride out to the Cross-J. He said no, said he had enemies in town that would like to catch him in open country, and that he didn't dare leave. I put him down as being slightly batty. While we were talking he glanced outside and saw another of Cassidy's farmers standing across the street — Nick somebody-or-other. I don't know his name. Seeing this Nick sort of threw a scare into Vincent, and he asked if there was any way he could leave my office without Nick seeing him. I took the cuss out the back door beyond the cells. That's the last I've seen of him. I certainly do wish, though, that those farmers get to scrapping among themselves. It might narrow down our problem some."

Johnny nodded. "Yeah, it would. I wish you'd kept this Jabez Vincent here until I came —"

"I thought of doing just that," Obie cut in. "Wish I had now. But I didn't really have anything to hold him on. Besides, I couldn't be sure but what he might be working some trick of Cassidy's, or something of the sort."

"You wouldn't be trying to avoid being sued for false arrest, would you?" Cal grinned.

Obie grew red. "To tell the truth, it did

occur to me," he confessed.

There was a sudden knock at the door. Obie raised his head and called, "Come on in."

The door opened. A slim, pale-faced young fellow with a scraggly beard and timid eyes slipped inside, glanced furtively in both directions along the street, then closed the door. He swayed a trifle as he came farther into the room.

"Here's your man now!" Obie exclaimed. "Johnny, this is Jabez Vincent."

"Glad to know you, Vincent." Johnny nodded. "My pal, here, is Cal Henry."

Vincent scarcely noticed the introduction. "You're Ranger Auburn, all right. That's all that matters to me."

"I've left the Rangers," Johnny said. "If it's a law officer you want, you'd better talk to Obie."

"I reckon you can tell me what I want to know," Vincent said, low-voiced. He hitched uncertainly at his bibbed overalls and pressed one hand to his left side, then again glanced furtively toward the window. "I'm afraid they'll get me," he gulped.

Obie rose quickly and blew out the flame in the lamp chimney. The office was plunged into darkness except for the faint light that entered from the street. Johnny stiffened for an attack of some kind, in case this was a trick, but apparently Vincent was genuinely frightened.

"What's on your mind, Vincent?" Johnny asked.

"I saw you out to the Cross-J yesterday," Vincent said in his timid tones. "I liked the way you handled things out there. I was against that wire-stringing right from the first, but Cassidy said I'd have to do my part or lose my money."

"What money?" from Johnny.

"My three hundred dollars I paid Ben Cassidy to get me a lease for a section of land. Things ain't like he said they would be at all."

"I imagine not," Johnny said kindly, "but I don't just understand. Let's start at the beginning. You aren't Texas stock."

"No, sir. I'm from Arkansas. Me and my wife had a little farm up there, but we always wanted to come to Texas. We sold out, and I give her half the money to live on while I come down to Texas to look the land over. It was in Dallas that I heard that Cassidy was working on some sort of land-development scheme. Feller in a saloon told me. I wanted in, so I looked up Cassidy. At first he told me he had all the men he wanted, but I mentioned I had three hundred dollars to put into a farm, and he got more friendly and agreed to let me come in. He brought us here —"

"You mean," Johnny asked, "that Cassidy agreed to sell you some land for three hundred dollars?"

227

"No sir. He just said he'd get me a lease from the state. Said there'd be plenty of water and that I could grow three crops of yams a year, if I wanted to, at the place he'd take us. That sounded better than anything I'd ever struck, and with a ninety-nine-year lease, I figured me'n Molly would be living in luxury when I brought her on. But it ain't worked out that way. I don't like these other farmers. They don't seem like real farmers to me. Some of them are right tough." He added plaintively, "Especially that Nick feller."

"I reckon they are," Johnny agreed.

"Last night," Vincent continued, "I told Nick I didn't like the way things was shaping up and that I calc'lated to ask your advice. He told me to stay away from you, but I slipped away from him. You'd left the Cross-J when I got there. Nick had followed me. On my way back from the Cross-J he took a couple of shots at me. Hit me too. But I whipped up my horse and come on to town. Since then I've been hiding where I could, but they've been hunting me all day —"

"You mean he wounded you?" Johnny cut in.

"Got me in the side. It ain't so bad, though, most of the time."

"Light up that lamp, Obie," Johnny said swiftly. "Cal, you stand by the door and see nobody comes near."

The room flared into light again. Vincent was still standing as before. "Dammit, man, sit down," Johnny said.

He forced Vincent down to a chair and ripped open his shirt. A bunch of bloody bandages met his eye. The bandages were none too clean. Johnny asked, "Who bandaged this for you?"

"I done it myself. I found those rags under the floor of the Maverick." Vincent forced a wan smile. "There's quite a space between the floor and the ground. I hid there most of the day when they were looking for me. Right above where I was laying is that back room of Malotte's, where Malotte and Tascosa and Cassidy sleep. I heard them talking and I knew they were fixing to have me killed."

"That's one more score against Cassidy," Johnny said shortly. "We'll remember that. Obie, have you got any clean rags and some water?"

"No rags, but I can furnish a towel that ain't been used." Obie set a pan of water and a clean towel on a near by chair.

By this time Johnny had the blood-soaked bandages removed. "You've lost a heap of blood, Vincent," he said.

"I reckon to make out if I can get a cup of coffee and a couple of slabs of bread. Ain't et since last night."

Johnny swore under his breath as he

bathed the wound and made a fresh bandage. "It's not too bad, Vincent," he said, pity in his voice. "There's a slug got to come out of your side. I could feel it under the skin. I reckon it's probably cracked a rib. But with some food and a good sleep you'll feel first-rate, once we get that bullet snaked out of your hide."

"I could sure use some sleep, but I ain't got a place, now —"

"Hell!" Obie broke in. "He can sleep here."

Johnny shook his head. "I'll take him down to my room at the hotel. Think you can make to walk that far if Cal and I help, Vincent?"

"Golly, yes. I feel better already. But what I wanted to see you about, Mister Auburn, is to ask a question. Is it lawful for Cassidy to keep the lease paper to my land after I've paid him my money?"

"You haven't the lease?" Johnny asked, surprised.

Vincent shook his head. "None of us have. Cassidy keeps all the leases, though they're made out in the different fellers' names. Today, when I was under the floor of the Maverick, hid there like a rabbit in its hole, I heard Cassidy say he'd own all the Painted Post Valley one of these days. And Malotte laughed and said maybe the whole county. And there was some more talk about how

230

Malotte could furnish as many leases as was needed."

Johnny frowned. "Malotte said that, eh?"

"Yes sir, he did. But I think I should have my lease paper, shouldn't I?"

Johnny scarcely heard the man. He turned slowly to Obie, standing near. "I think we've hit something."

"Meaning what?" Obie asked.

"The first clue to Cassidy's game."

"Meaning what?" Obie said again.

"I'll tell you when I get it all worked out in my own mind, Obie. . . . Yes, Vincent, you should have your lease paper. I promise that you'll get your section too. It may not be the land of milk and honey that Cassidy pictured it when he took your three hundred dollars, but it will be right good land. Right now forget it. We'll get down to my hotel and we'll talk some more there. Obie, when we leave, you see can you rustle up some food and hot coffee someplace and bring it to the hotel." He raised his voice. "Cal, lend a hand. Vincent is sort of shaky on his pins. We'll help him walk down to my room."

They left Obie's office, and ten minutes later Johnny was arousing the sleepy-eyed night clerk in the hotel. "Friend of mine," Johnny explained briefly and passed through the tiny lobby, down the hall, and into his room after he had unlocked the door. Cal struck a match and lighted the oil lamp.

231

"How do you feel now, Vincent?" Johnny asked.

Vincent dropped rather heavily into a chair. "Kind of lightheaded." He grinned foolishly. "But I'm a heap better just since I talked to you —"

"Catch him!" Cal exclaimed suddenly as Vincent started to topple from the chair. But Johnny had already put out his hand and prevented Vincent from falling. Next he noticed that Vincent's shirt was stained with a rapidly spreading crimson.

"Dammit!" Johnny growled. "That wound has broke out again." He half carried Vincent to the bed and stretched him out, full length, then opened his shirt for the second time. The fresh towel that Obie had furnished was already soaked with bright red wetness. Johnny glanced at Vincent. The man's eyes were closed. He had fainted.

"I don't like this," Johnny said troubledly. "Cal, you light a shuck out of here as fast as you can and bring back a doctor."

"Doc Kilburn's the best."

"Get him, then. I don't want this kid to bleed to death." Cal left in a hurry. Johnny turned back to the ashen-faced Vincent and did what he could to stop the flow of blood. "Maybe," he muttered, "this isn't as serious as it looks, but I don't like to run chances. Maybe he just fainted from lack of blood and food and sleep. I've seen similar wounds that didn't bleed this bad, though."

He stepped to a near-by rack and got a fresh towel. Five minutes passed. Johnny sighed with relief. The wound didn't seem to be bleeding so freely now.

Vincent stirred and opened his eyes. "Wha-what happened?" he asked weakly.

"It's all right, old-timer." Johnny smiled. "You just passed out for a while. I've sent for a doctor. He'll fix you up pronto, and if Obie ever gets here with some grub and hot coffee you'll be able to write your wife that you're feeling better than you ever did in your life."

"I sure hope so." Already the man seemed to be stronger again. He wanted to sit up, so Johnny braced him with a couple of pillows behind his back.

"No, you'd better stay on the bed," Johnny advised. "You don't want to stir around too much."

At that moment Cal returned with news that Dr. Kilburn would arrive as soon as he could get his clothes on. Cal was panting heavily. "I sure wouldn't never make a runner" — he grinned — "but I got to admit I made the distance from here to Doc's and back again in nothing flat." He dropped into a chair in one corner, long legs stretched out before him.

Johnny examined the towel, then, with the intention of wringing it out in a basin of water, he stepped back from the bed. At that instant it happened:

There came the sharp crashing of window glass. From the alley outside sounded the rattle of firearms. Jabez Vincent sat bolt upright, then dropped back with a long tired sigh. In one swift movement Johnny extinguished the flame in the lamp chimney, plunging the room into utter darkness. Running footsteps clumped along the alley.

XXII. Powder Smoke

For just an instant there was silence in the room; then Johnny asked, "You all right, Cal?"

"I was out of sight from that window. You?"

"Missed me as I stepped back from the bed. Come on!"

Obie's startled voice sounded in the hall outside. "What the hell's going on?"

He swung open the door as Cal started forward, colliding with him. The two men went to the floor. An odor of spilled coffee swept through the room. There was considerable swearing as the pair climbed to their feet.

Johnny was at the window, raising the frame with its shattered glass. He leaped outside, calling back: "They got Vincent. Come on, you clumsy-footed galoots!"

He was already running swiftly along the alley, a gun in either fist. Behind him he heard Cal and Obie tumbling from the window. Ahead, running footsteps sounded. Johnny could dimly make out several forms. One of the forms stopped. Gunfire exploded redly. Johnny heard the savage whine as the bullet passed overhead. He thumbed a shot from his right gun, then from his left. At almost the same instant, behind him, Cal and Obie cut loose with their six-shooters.

From up ahead came more shooting. Powder smoke swirled through the alley. The fleeing assailants had too much of a lead to be caught. Once they'd reached the next cross street they could scatter and lose themselves in the town. Again Johnny sent slim lances of flame spurting from his six-shooters. A sharp cry of pain reached his ears; then came the sound of a falling body. "Got one of them," he panted.

In the faint light at the next street intersection he caught a momentary glimpse of three swiftly running forms just before they disappeared from sight. Reluctantly he slowed his steps, and Cal and Obie overtook him.

"Giving up the chase?" Cal asked disappointedly.

"We'd never catch 'em now," Johnny said. "I think I got one of the scuts, though — just a mite farther ahead."

They moved on, searching the dark alley with sharp eyes. From Chisholm Street they could hear the excited shouts of men attracted by the noise of the shooting. Several steps farther on they found the man Johnny had downed. He was breathing with difficulty, stretched flat on his back; a soft bubbling noise issued from his throat.

They knelt at his side. Obie scratched a match. "I know this scut!" he exclaimed an instant later. "One of Cassidy's farmers. It's the hombre they call Nick."

The man was dying fast. Johnny put his lips close to the fellow's ear. "Who else was with you?" he asked.

For a moment there was no answer; then Nick spoke, so faintly Johnny could scarcely hear him. "Tascosa Jake — and — and —" And then he died. Obie's match flickered out.

Johnny got to his feet. "That's all," he said grimly. "Tough he couldn't have lived a minute longer. But we've got one name, anyway. Obie, you and Cal better get back to the hotel."

"Where you going?" Obie asked.

"To the Maverick. I want Tascosa. I keep thinking of that poor Vincent kid and his wife waiting for him up in Arkansas."

"I'll go with you," Cal said promptly.

"All right," Johnny consented. "But I don't want you taking a hand unless somebody else cuts in —"

"Hey," Obie protested, "I'm sheriff here. You'd better let me arrest Tascosa."

Johnny shook his head. "This is my job."

"The hell it is," Obie growled and started walking down the alley.

"Where you going?" Johnny asked.

"To the Maverick," Obie snapped. "If you're coming you'd better hurry up."

Johnny laughed grimly. "Of all the mule-stubborn hombres I ever saw —"

"Stubborn, my foot!" Obie ejaculated, striding along ahead. "I just don't aim to be left out of any more doings. If Cal can go along, so can I. Who in hell's got a better right? I'm sheriff, ain't I?"

"You're sheriff," Johnny surrendered. "Come on, Cal, we'll let him go with us."

"You can't prevent me from going," Obie grunted.

They strode along, side by side, reloading guns as they moved. Turning west on Bowie Street, at the end of the alley, they made their way to Chisholm and thence to the Maverick Saloon. There were a great many people on the street by this time, drawn out by the sounds of the shooting, but Obie refused to answer any questions. Reaching the Maverick, they pushed inside, to find only Cold-Deck and Cassidy standing at the bar. Everybody else had rushed outside by this time.

"What is this, a delegation?" Cassidy greeted lightly. "Sheriff, I understand there was some shooting. Just so there won't be any misunderstandings — or false arrests — I've got proof that I've not left this bar in some time."

Johnny snapped. "Where's Tascosa Jake?"

Cassidy shrugged. "How should I know where he is? I'm not keeping cases on him."

Johnny drew one gun, brushed past Malotte and Cassidy, jerked open a door at the rear. The room beyond the door held only three cots, a table, and some chairs. There was no sign of Tascosa. Johnny returned to the barroom.

Cold-Deck sneered. "You interested in my back room?"

"Only as a nest for skunks," Johnny said coldly. "The nest seems empty at present, but the skunks aren't far off. I can smell 'em."

"Now, you look here, Auburn —" Malotte commenced angrily.

"Shut your face before I hammer it shut with my gun barrel," Johnny snapped. Malotte gulped and kept quiet. Johnny turned to Cassidy. "Jabez Vincent was killed tonight by Tascosa and three other men. One of the coyotes was named Nick. He's lying dead in the alley between Chisholm and Comanche streets. The rest got away —"

"Just a minute," Cassidy interrupted. "What makes you so sure Tascosa was mixed into the game?"

"Nick named him before he died."

Cassidy shrugged. "I don't know a damn thing about it. I don't know where Tascosa is, but I don't reckon he killed anybody. He'll shoot, yes, if he has to, but he don't run

239

when he's done a job."

"He does when Johnny is on his trail, I'll bet," Obie said angrily.

"That's your idea," Cassidy said coldly. "I've told you I don't know anything about it. I don't even know this Vincent you mentioned."

"You're a liar!" Johnny said flatly.

Cassidy flushed but held his temper. "You tell me who he is, then," he challenged.

"He's that young farmer kid who paid you three hundred for a lease —"

"Hell! Those farmers are always fighting among themselves," Cassidy said nastily, then paused. "What's that about me taking three hundred for a lease?"

"I had Vincent's word on it," Johnny said.

"He lied like hell," Cassidy growled. "Now that you mention it, I do remember a skinny young hoe man named Vincent, but I never got any money from him. He come around begging me to bring him here —"

"I thought you maintained you had nothing to do with bringing those farmers into this country," Johnny flashed.

Cassidy opened his mouth to reply, then remained silent. To cover his pardner's confusion, Cold-Deck Malotte cut in with, "Look, I got certain rights. This is my saloon. We've told you we know nothing about Vincent, or Tascosa's whereabouts. Suppose you hombres get out and let us drink in peace."

"Malotte," Johnny said, "how would you like to have all your teeth knocked down your throat? You're sure breeding a bruise talking that-a-way. Sure, this is your saloon. I'm looking forward to the day when it will be sold —"

"Ain't planning to sell —" Malotte commenced sullenly.

"It's my planning," Johnny said coldly. "You aren't going to have anything to do with it, Malotte. I keep thinking about young Vincent's wife waiting for him up in Arkansas. She could use three hundred dollars — and more than that. Eventually I aim to see that she gets it."

"Now, you look here, Auburn" — Cassidy had found his tongue again — "we don't want trouble with you, but —"

Johnny said, "Oh hell," in a disgusted tone and turned to Cal and Obie. "Come on, let's drift out of this dump." They nodded, and he turned back to Cassidy and Malotte. "Tell Tascosa for me that I'm on his trail. Tell him to keep his gun in a loose holster. Tell him I'd sure like to see him coming hunting me — but he'd better come with his guns a-smoking!"

He turned and left the saloon, followed by Cal and Obie. On the street he said, "Nothing more to be found there. Cassidy had his alibi all ready. I'll catch Tascosa yet, someplace."

They returned to the hotel. In the lobby they found the clerk talking to Dr. Kilburn, a spare, gray-haired man who looked to be the typical frontier physician.

The hotel clerk said, "I moved your things to another room, Mr. Auburn."

Johnny nodded, said to the doctor, "No chance for Vincent, eh?"

Kilburn shook his head. "He died instantly."

Johnny said, "I figured as much when the shots crashed through my window, but I couldn't take time to make sure. We got one of the skunks that did the shooting."

"That's good," Kilburn said. He prepared to take his departure, then spoke to Obie. "The undertaker is back there getting Vincent's body now."

"He got here fast," Johnny commented.

Kilburn smiled grimly. "This particular undertaker is fast. Every time he hears a shot he takes down his bottle of embalming fluid and grabs his hat. Half the time he don't even stop for his hat."

Obie said, "I'll go tell him he's got another job out in the alley."

"He already heard about it," Kilburn said. "Well, good night, gentlemen."

He left the hotel lobby. Johnny said, "Come on, Cal, let's go put up our horses; then we'll come back and turn in. You can sleep in my room."

242

They left the hotel, accompanied by Obie. Obie said as their steps sounded along the plank sidewalks, "Business has sure been brisk lately. I reckon I'll have to polish up my badge."

Johnny was still seething inside at the thought of young Vincent's brutal murder. "Don't go buying your polish in too much of a hurry," he said grimly. "Before I get through with this town I'm figuring to make it so peaceful that badges won't be necessary."

XXIII. Challenge!

The following morning after breakfast at the Texas Café, Obie said, "What you got lined up for today, Johnny? Anything special?"

"Anything that Johnny lines up will be special." Cal grinned.

Johnny looked thoughtful. "I've got one or two things in mind," he confessed. "Of course right now I'm more interested in finding Tascosa Jake Wiley than in anything else."

The three men were standing out in front of the restaurant, smoking cigarettes. Bright morning sun shone along the main street. A few horses stood at hitch racks along the way. Pedestrians moved at an easy gait on either side of Chisholm Street or lounged in the deep shadow beneath the wooden awnings that fronted the various stores. It was going to be hot when the sun rose higher.

Johnny continued, "Of course we could start in and make a search for Tascosa, but I figure that would just be a waste of time. If we'll just take it easy I think he'll come into the open eventually. Regardless what you may think of the man, he's got nerve. Too much nerve to run out of town, in my estimation. And Cassidy is going to have to force him into the open or admit that he's licked. The other night, down in the Maverick, I outnerved him to some extent, but men like Tascosa will stick and shoot it out, in the long run, rather than show the white feather. With Tascosa feeling like I think he does, and with Malotte and Cassidy to do a bit of prodding, Tascosa will show up again after he's primed his courage with a few drinks."

Cal nodded. "I reckon you got him sized up about right, Johnny."

Obie looked uneasy. "I wish I knew where the scut was right now. I'd put him under arrest."

"I'd rather you didn't," Johnny observed quietly. "Tascosa's my meat. I'm asking that you don't interfere, Obie."

"I don't know," Obie said dubiously. "I know Tascosa. Sure, he'll have a few drinks before he goes into a gunfight, but it won't unsettle his aim any. It'll make him sharper, if anything. If Tascosa gets a chance to pick his own time to meet you, Johnny, he'll feel that he's got the advantage — and he won't come into the open until he's sure he's right."

Johnny pondered the situation. "Maybe we can force him into the open," he said at last. "Look, here's an idea that might work. You two circulate around town and spread this idea as much as you can."

"What idea?" Obie asked.

Johnny explained: "Just tell folks that I'm going to ride to Fritada this afternoon to wire a description of Tascosa to the Texas Rangers and all other law officers in the state. Let on like I'm working them up to a statewide search for Tascosa —"

"You going to do that?" Obie's eyes widened.

Johnny shook his head. "I don't reckon that will be necessary. But eventually the word will reach Cassidy and Malotte. They know where Tascosa is hiding out, all right. They'll send the word to him and —"

"Smart, very, very smart," Cal said admiringly.

"How so?" Obie frowned.

Johnny said, "I figure when Tascosa hears the news he'll try to stop me from reaching Fritada. To do that he's got to come into the open. Get the idea, Obie?"

Obie nodded slowly. "It might work."

"It'll sure as hell work, I'm betting," Cal insisted.

Johnny nodded. "All right, get busy, you two, and circulate the story. Oh, by the way, Obie, you still got those N.E.P. shells that Cassidy threw away that day? If so, I'd like to get a couple of them."

"Sure, they're still on the desk in my office. The door's unlocked. Go in and help yourself." Obie looked surprised, "What you want them for?"

"I got an idea. It might work and it might not. I'll let you in on it when I know for sure," Johnny replied. "Well, get going, pards. I'll see you later."

He watched the two separate and head off down the street. For a few minutes Johnny stood there, thoughtfully drawing on his cigarette. Then he tossed down the butt, ground it under his toe, and sauntered off in the direction of the sheriff's office.

Ten minutes later he was entering Eli Smith's General Store. It was still too early for many customers, and Smith himself edged up to the counter to ask Johnny what was required.

Johnny rolled a couple of cartridges on the counter. "Got any more of these, Mr. Smith?"

Smith picked up one of the cartridges and squinted at it through his spectacles. "N.E.P. load, eh?" he commented. "Yes sir, I got part of one box left. You want 'em? Let you have 'em dirt cheap."

"Just part of a box?" Johnny asked. "No more?"

"That's all. And you won't find any more in town, either. To be frank with you, Mister Auburn, I'd rather not sell 'em to you. They just ain't no good. A salesman sold me on the idea of putting some in stock. He

247

bragged on his N.E.P. ca'tridges all over the place, but I'm glad I only took one box. I was a fool to do that. I reckon every other storekeeper in town had better sense than me, 'cause nobody else brought any."

"Yours was the only box in Painted Post, eh?"

"That's right."

"Haven't you ever sold any?"

"Sold what's missing from my box, but that's all."

"Who bought 'em?" Johnny held his breath, waiting for the reply, fearing that Smith might not remember.

"Ben Cassidy bought a handful. He came in one day, looking for regular Colt's ca'tridges, but I was plumb out of stock. All I had on hand was the N.E.P.'s. I told him what the salesman claimed for 'em, and Ben allowed as how he'd try 'em out. Next time Ben came in he said they were next to lousy and could he get some Colt loads. He was pretty disgusted all right —"

"And you never sold any to anybody else?" Johnny asked narrowly.

"Ain't I just told you? Nope, Ben Cassidy is the only man in this town that ever had N.E.P.'s, 'cause I sold him the only ones that were to be had in Painted Post, and I never sold any to anybody else."

Johnny smiled. "Thanks a lot. If you say the N.E.P. loads are no good, that's enough for me. I don't want any either." He shoved the two cartridges he had carried in across the counter. "Put these in your box. Maybe that salesman will show up again someday and you can get a refund."

"I'd like to sell you some Colt ca'tridges."

"I'll drop in and get 'em when I've got more time."

Johnny left the store and stepped to the street, a glint of extreme satisfaction showing in his eyes. "That settles one thing, anyway," he mused. "It's commencing to look as if the noose is drawing a little tighter around Ben Cassidy's neck."

Johnny drifted around town for a while, bumped into Obie and Cal now and then, and learned they were spreading the story he had fabricated. About ten o'clock he dropped into Urban Everett's bar for a bottle of cold beer, took it to a table at one side, and quenched his thirst while he perused a week-old copy of a San Antonio newspaper. At eleven-thirty he rose and headed in the direction of the sheriff's office. Obie and Cal were already waiting for him there. Both looked disappointed as they stood there on the office porch.

"I'm afraid it's not going to work," Cal said. "The whole morning has passed and no sign of Tascosa yet. I personally told Cassidy —"

"How'd he take it?" Johnny asked.

"He looked sort of shocked at first; then he smiled, shrugged his shoulders, and said it was no concern of his."

"And I told Malotte," Obie put in. "I met him coming out of the Texas Café. He looked sort of worried, but he acted about the same as Cal says Cassidy did. I reckon you'll have to think up something else, Johnny."

Johnny said confidently, "The day isn't over yet. Lots of times rattlers don't come out of their holes until sundown."

Nobody said anything more for a few minutes. With so much to occupy their minds, they found relief in fashioning and lighting cigarettes. By this time they had dropped into straight-backed chairs tilted against the wall. Obie stared moodily down the street, drawing deeply on his smoke.

One of Cassidy's farmers left the Maverick Saloon, walked north along Chisholm Street, and then crossed over as he drew near the sheriff's office. He came directly to Johnny, one stubby-fingered hand holding out a folded sheet of note paper. "For you, Auburn," he said contemptuously. "I'm to wait for an answer."

Johnny took the note, unfolded it, read the words written there. An icy smile twitched the corners of his mouth. He glanced up at the waiting farmer. "Tell him I'll be there," he said shortly.

The farmer nodded and set off at a faster gait on his return to the Maverick.

Obie and Cal looked after him a minute; then Obie turned to Johnny. "Tell who you'll be where?" he blurted.

Johnny held the note so they could both see it. It read:

AUBURN:

I'll leave the Maverick Saloon at 12:00 o'clock and walk toward the Cash Deal. You been looking for me. I'll come to meet you, if you got the guts to face my guns. Otherwise, get out of Painted Post or I'll kill you on sight.

TASCOSA JAKE WILEY

"The rattler," Johnny said softly, rising to his feet, "has emerged from its hole, rattling a challenge. The scheme worked, pards. We drew him into the open. The time has come. I aim to meet that challenge!"

XXIV. Blood in the Dust

Johnny drew out his watch, noted the time. "I'll be starting presently," he said.

"Look here," Cal exclaimed. "I reckon I'd better go along. This might be some trick. Maybe Cassidy or Malotte is hidden along the street —"

"I don't reckon so," Johnny cut in. "Tascosa's reputation is at stake. I know his type right well. He wants the rep of being able to say he outfoxed me, outshot me, all by himself. If I had to face more than one, that might bring in the law. Obie could take steps —"

"I don't know but what I ought to interfere as it is," Obie interrupted dubiously. "I'm sworn to prevent fights, not watch them. It seems to me my duty —"

"Your duty," Johnny said swiftly, "is to do everything possible to bring peace to this country. Sure, Obie, you've got the right to stop this fight here and now. I'm asking you not to do it. Oh, you could put us both — Tascosa and me — under bond to keep the peace, but what would it mean?" He answered his own question: "Simply that this feud would flare out some other day. Painted Post isn't big enough to hold both Tascosa and me. One of us has to leave. The less you do to prevent things coming to a head, the better off it will be all around. I'm just asking one thing, Obie; don't interfere."

"But dammit, Johnny," Obie protested, "I'm afraid Tascosa will pull some trick. Even if he didn't, he's good; make no mistake about that. He's picked his own time for the fight. That means he's confident. Hell's bells, Johnny! I don't like it."

"Neither do I," Johnny said soberly. "No decent man likes killing, but there comes a time when that's the only way to get rid of a mad dog."

"But why you?" Obie persisted. "Why isn't it my job?"

"Because," Johnny said bluntly, "I don't think you'd have a chance against Tascosa's guns, Obie. That's one reason. The other: Tascosa's my meat. He's my job. All I ask from you is to keep hands off." He consulted his watch again. "One minute to twelve. You and Cal wait here. I'll be back shortly — I hope."

He shook hands with the two, then pulled out his six-shooters one by one, spun the cylinders, and shoved the guns back into holsters. Then he stepped out to the middle of the street and started walking in the direction of the Cash Deal. Glancing south two blocks along Chisholm Street, Johnny saw Tascosa just leaving the Maverick. Tascosa, too, took the middle-of-the-road course.

"He had it figured about right," Johnny mused. "One block's walk for each of us should bring us together just about opposite the Cash Deal."

He strode on, his boots kicking up small dust clouds as he moved. He wasn't hurrying. Just walking free and easy, arms swinging at his sides, fingertips brushing the wood of his gun butts as they moved past.

It was blazing hot along Chisholm. The street seemed strangely empty and deserted, but Johnny could sense the peering eyes watching him from doorways and from behind windows. News of the fight had spread like wildfire through the town, it was plainly apparent. Even horses and wagons had been moved off the thoroughfare: stray bullets can sometimes do a vast amount of damage.

Tascosa was much easier to distinguish by this time. He, too, was taking his time. Hurrying might mean unsteady nerves. Unsteady nerves caused poor shooting.

There didn't seem to be a sound along the street. A hot wind blowing in from the open range fanned Johnny's cheeks and lifted small swirls of dust in the roadway.

Step by step by step the two men came closer to each other. Still neither had made a move to draw his guns. The corner of Chisholm and Bowie, where the Cash Deal Saloon was located, wasn't more than a quarter of a block away now.

A man's voice called from a store doorway, "Go get him, Ranger!"

Johnny nodded without turning his head to see who had spoken. Now he didn't dare remove his gaze from Tascosa's rapidly approaching figure as Tascosa broke into a quicker gait. Johnny continued at the same even walk.

"He's getting anxious," Johnny told himself, and a moment later, "That wind's with him. I'll have to figure on that." He was watching Tascosa's swinging hands closely now, expecting every minute to see them dart toward holsters. But Tascosa failed to make the expected move.

"Anxious, mebbe," Johnny muttered, "but he's not letting it sway his judgment. He likes to get in close. Waiting for me to make the first move, mebbe. I'm danged if I will!"

He could see Tascosa's features clearly by this time. He wondered if the man ever would reach for six-shooters, but Tascosa's hands were staying well wide of his guns.

And then a momentary pause in the man's stride tipped off Johnny that something was coming. Tascosa's right hand shot up. Swift spurts of fire burst from that hand even as Johnny took two quick sidewise steps. He heard the whine of lead past his body and knew the first attempt had failed.

"Underarm gun!" Johnny exclaimed. "He thought he'd take me by surprise while I was watching his holsters."

He heard Tascosa's angry curse as the man flung the hidden gun to one side and reached for his six-shooters. But Johnny's guns were already out, belching lead and smoke and red flame.

He saw dust jump from Tascosa's vest as a bullet struck savagely through the cloth. Tascosa swayed back, left arm dangling uselessly by his side, but managed to keep his feet. He lifted his right gun as Johnny broke into a run and came charging in close, thumbing swift shots as he moved.

Unsteadily Tascosa dropped to one knee, resting his gun hand along his leg. Flame spurted again from Johnny's guns, and Tascosa's final shot flew high and to one side. The six-shooter dropped from his hand as he fought to keep in an erect position. Then quite suddenly he rolled to one shoulder and sprawled in the roadway.

Guns alert for more tricks, Johnny advanced warily. But it was no trick this time. Tascosa breathed his last even as Johnny approached. Johnny stood over him a moment, seeing the blood drip swiftly to the dust below that huddled form; then he turned away and methodically commenced reloading his guns.

A great shout echoed along Chisholm Street. Men poured into the roadway and gathered around Johnny and the dead Tascosa. The first to reach Johnny was Cal; Obie was close behind.

"You hurt any, Johnny?" Cal asked.

"Not any," Johnny replied quietly. "How'd you get here so quick?"

Obie supplied the answer to that one. "We followed along behind you, hugging close to the store fronts so you wouldn't spot us."

"I wasn't looking behind me any," Johnny said. "I had a job to do ahead."

"You sure done it up brown," Obie declared.

Several men crowded around, congratulating Johnny and offering to buy him drinks. Johnny refused. "Let's get out of this," he said to Obie and Cal.

They started away; then Johnny's gaze fell on Ben Cassidy pushing up with Malotte on his heels. Malotte looked white as a sheet. Cassidy met Johnny's eyes, nodded shortly. "I see you found Tascosa," he commented coolly. "I told you once I didn't know where he was. Where'd you find him?"

"Saw him leaving the Maverick not so long ago." Johnny smiled thinly. "I suppose you and Malotte don't know anything about that."

"We haven't been in the Maverick the last hour or so," Malotte said. His voice sounded shaky.

"So you can't connect me with this," Cassidy sneered.

Johnny laughed contemptuously. "Tascosa had a hideout gun, Cassidy. The trick didn't work, but it did smell almightily of your scheming. Now I don't give a damn if you knew where he was or not. I got him and I'll get you and Malotte the same way. You'd better think it over and decide to move. My patience is plumb at an end."

"But look here, Auburn," Cassidy commenced, "you can't run us out of town."

"Yes, I could," Johnny snapped, "but I'm not going to try very hard. I'm hoping you'll stay. I'm just giving you fair warning, that's all." He turned to Cal and Obie. "Come on, let's get away from here. I've made my talk. It's Cassidy's next play!"

XXV. Blaine Makes a Report

Three weeks passed, during which the excitement over the fight between Johnny and Tascosa Jake Wiley gradually subsided. Cassidy denied all and every accusation that he had had any connection with the gun duel, though Johnny felt certain the use of the underarm gun had been Cassidy's idea. However, Johnny considered, it didn't greatly matter now.

A period of peaceful inactivity had set in, while Johnny chafed restlessly at the delay in his plans; however, he couldn't take any further steps until such time as Sam Blaine had finished his surveying job. Several times Johnny had been tempted to ride out and find Blaine and his crew and see if he couldn't urge them along to a swifter conclusion of the task, but sober second thought convinced Johnny that Blaine knew his business and wouldn't waste any time finishing up.

Apparently, Cassidy, also, had been doing some worrying about the surveying. He stopped Johnny on the street one day and asked rather humbly if he might speak to him.

"Nothing to prevent that I know of," Johnny said coldly, his eyes boring into Cassidy's. "What's on your mind?"

"I'm just wondering," Cassidy said uneasily, "when that surveyor you brought here is going to get around to measuring up the various sections called for on the leases of the farmers. They'd like to know where they stand. Course some of them have paced off the distances and put up their fences, figuring it will save time in the long run, even if they do have to shift lines a mite —"

"Cassidy," Johnny broke in, "for a man who claims he didn't bring those farmers here, you sure show a heap of interest in their doings."

"I got a personal interest in it now. You see" — Cassidy hesitated awkwardly — "I took over Rufe Howard's lease after you finished him off. Between you and me, I was glad to see Howard rubbed out. He was quarrelsome and no good."

"That seems to be your attitude on every one of your men that have been put out of the game, Cassidy," Johnny said. "You sure change your mind quick — after your pals are no longer of any use to you."

"Dammit!" Cassidy exclaimed angrily. "They're not my men. You're mistaken about me, Johnny. I'd like to be friends with you. I realize you took my part against Jenkins when you first come here and stopped him cutting our wire."

"I didn't take your part" — Johnny shook his head — "the law did. I merely enforced the law when I was a Ranger. And you and I can't ever be friends, Cassidy. I quit the Rangers simply so I could have a free hand in settling your hash. I hope that's clear."

"You're making a mistake, Auburn." Cassidy kept his temper, but his voice held a threatening note.

"You've already made one," Johnny retorted. "I'm going to make you realize that fact before I get through with you. So far as that surveyor is concerned, I'm just as anxious as you to get things settled here, but as I told you before, there can't much be done until the whole valley has been surveyed and boundary lines established. That answers your question."

And without waiting for Cassidy to reply Johnny walked on. Cassidy stood looking after him a few minutes, hate burning in his eyes. "Oh, I'll get you yet, Auburn," he promised himself savagely, "and when I get you I'll get you right."

The days had passed pleasantly enough for Johnny. He had taken rides with Pat, thus further cementing their "friendship," as they called it. Johnny and Cal had also traveled through the valley, checking into the so-called farmers' activities.

Not many of the Cassidy gang apparently had made a very serious effort to get their places, as they expected them to be, in order. Fences that had been cut by the Cross-J weeks before still remained unrepaired. Nowhere could Johnny and Cal see that any attempt at farming had been made. The men were living in covered wagons and tents; none of them had started building a house, though timber was plentiful on the hills. Whenever Johnny and Cal came on them unexpectedly they seemed to be just loafing around, eating, and drinking. Some of them had slatternly women with them, and while they greeted Johnny and Cal sullenly, it was plain to be seen they were enjoying the life.

Johnny and Cal had pulled out of one of these typical camps one day when Cal commented, "Farmers, hell! I can respect a hardworking sodbuster, but these hombres scattered through the valley aren't farmers. I ain't seen one yet that had any plowing done. If you ask me, they're just holding this land for Cassidy."

"That was my guess a long spell back." Johnny nodded.

"But when are we going to get them out of here?"

"I wish I knew. A heap depends on Sam Blaine. I can't move until I hear from him."

"Why?"

Johnny smiled. "Cal, you're going to have to take my word that this will pan out all right, but until things are lined up more to my liking I don't like to tell what I know."

"You mean there's a chance that your plan won't work out?"

"I never count on anything until I've got it right in my grasp. The odds are with us, but I'm just sort of superstitious about telling what I know until things are settled. Now don't get an idea I don't trust you. I do — from the ground up — but there's always the chance of a fellow getting sick or shot and becoming delirious and talking too much. See what I mean?"

"Sure, sure, Johnny."

"I'll tell you what, Cal," Johnny promised. "Once things are settled, you'll be the first I'll tell."

"Aw, forget it." Cal grinned. "Y'know, I kind of had an idea that privilege was being reserved for somebody else — a friend of yours named Pat."

"Maybe that'll be your job. When things once break, this town will be busted wide open. I'll be moving fast and won't be able to spare the time to make a ride to the Cross-J. Between you and me, I've got enough on Cassidy right now to put a noose around his neck, but that's only part of the business. I don't want any tag ends to be gathered later. I want to wash everything up at once. Lord A'mighty! How I do wish I'd hear from Blaine."

Three days later Johnny got his wish. He

was sitting on the porch of the Cash Deal Saloon when Blaine came loping his pony into town. The horse was streaked with perspiration and foam, showing that Blaine had pushed it hard. He pulled to a stop at the hitch rack and hurried up on the porch, grinning as he noted Johnny's expectant features.

"It's all right, Johnny; we're finished." He relieved Johnny's feelings at once.

"Lord, I'm glad to see you!" Johnny exclaimed. "Everything all right, eh?"

Blaine slapped a bulky package of papers in his pocket. "It's all here — measurements, boundaries, established corners — everything."

"Pretty big job, eh?"

"It'd have been a lot worse if we'd been surveying fresh ground. As it was, all we had to do was check on the lines and figures made by Sam Houston's men."

"Where's your crew?"

"The outfit will be along eventually. I pushed ahead as fast as possible. I knew you were in a hurry."

"I'm sure obliged to you, Sam. You must be thirsty. Let's go inside for a drink."

"It'll have to be a fast one, then, if you're still anxious to get this business put on the ice. That's why I hurried. If you'll saddle up we can ride to Fritada in time to catch a train for Fort Worth, then make the jump to Austin."

"We'll do it." Johnny nodded eagerly. "The sooner I can get to the land office in the capital, the better I'll like it."

Fifteen minutes later Ben Cassidy, standing on the porch of the Maverick Saloon, saw Johnny and Blaine thundering past on their ponies, riding south out of town.

Cassidy drew thoughtfully on his cigar. "Now where they heading?" he mused uneasily. "Reckon I'll drift down to the Cash Deal and do some roundabout questioning."

He left the Maverick porch and walked swiftly in the direction of Urban Everett's saloon. Here, through the medium of a few well-placed questions, he learned that Johnny Auburn and a surveyor named Sam Blaine had left for Fritada. Urban didn't know, or wouldn't say, what their business was. But the single word "surveyor" awakened a swift train of suspicions in Cassidy's nimble mind.

He left the Cash Deal almost at a run and hurried back to the Maverick, where he called Cold-Deck Malotte out on the porch to tell him what he had learned.

Malotte looked blankly at his chief. "I don't see anything to get excited about," he commented in puzzled tones.

"*You* wouldn't!" Cassidy exclaimed disgustedly. "Look, Cold-Deck, those two have headed for Fritada. There's a Texas & Pacific train comes through just about the time they'll get there. Unless I miss my guess they're traveling to Austin to the land office."

"Why?"

"Why?" Cassidy almost shouted. "That's what I want to know. I've got a hunch Auburn has tricked us someway. I don't like the looks of things. If they ever get messing around that land office at the capital and start checking into leases we're sunk."

Malotte turned a shade whiter. He sank rather weakly into a near-by chair. "For God's sake, don't say that."

"I am saying it," Cassidy snapped. "I don't believe Auburn ever intended to survey the land our leases called for. But there was surveying done and —"

"Look, Ben" — Malotte had a sudden idea — "you don't suppose, do you, that Auburn has had the valley surveyed and is now riding to Austin to buy the whole property from the state?"

"Don't be a fool, Cold-Deck," Cassidy said roughly. "Do you know what Texas property — open range — is worth today?"

"Do you?"

"I know this much. That red granite capitol building they're putting up in Austin at present is figured to cost around three million dollars. The state gave three million acres of land to pay the cost. That makes open range worth a dollar an acre — in big lots, mind you —"

Malotte laughed scornfully. "Only a fool

266

would pay that much. Geez! A dollar an acre! Are you crazy?"

"I didn't set the price. But that gives you an idea what land is worth. All right, figure it out. There's roughly close to a hundred thousand acres of land in the Cross-J property. At current values that makes a hundred thousand dollars. Do you think Auburn, or Jenkins, or anybody else around here has that much money? Certainly not. So you can forget that idea about Auburn buying the property."

"I guess you're right," Malotte sighed. "But what did Auburn leave for Austin for?"

"That's what you're going to find out."

"Me?"

"You! There's a freight comes through Fritada in about an hour and a half. By riding hard you can catch it. They'll stop for you and sell you passage in the caboose. Probably you can get to Austin almost as soon as Auburn. Don't let him see you, but you work harder than you ever worked in your life. Find out what he's doing there."

"But — but —" Malotte gasped. "I can't leave my bar —"

"Louie can run the Maverick while you're gone. I'll be here to see that nothing goes wrong. Go on, get going now. While you're down to the livery getting your horse I'll go in and explain things to Louie."

There were further protestations on

Malotte's part, but in the end Cassidy had his way. Reluctantly Malotte started off toward the livery stable.

XXVI. The Noose Tightens

Four days later Johnny rode Cherokee into Painted Post. Man and rider were covered with dust and sweat; the little buckskin had covered the distance from Fritada in a time nothing short of miraculous. The first man Johnny saw was Cal Henry, seated on the porch of the Cash Deal with a bottle of beer in his hand.

"You're back!" Cal exclaimed, rising to his feet, a welcoming grin on his features.

"You're a-whooping I'm back!" Johnny exclaimed gleefully. He jerked the bottle of beer from Cal's hand. "I need that worse than you do. We'll get more later. But there's business first."

"Why, you crazy ranny," Cal chuckled. "You act like you'd gone crazy with the heat, or something."

Johnny lowered the bottle and chucked it to one side. His eyes bubbled with merriment. "Get this through your thick skull." He laughed. "We've saved the Cross-J for Alex Jenkins! I want you to ride your head off and break the news to him — and Pat. Here, take a look at this." He jerked a long envelope from his pocket and handed it to Cal. Cal drew out the pages it contained, glanced at them, then stared at Johnny with dawning amazement in his eyes.

"Why — why," he stammered, for once at a loss for words, "this is a deed for the whole Painted Post Valley, as I understood it, made out to Alex —"

"Right, and all duly recorded," Johnny enthused, "in the name of Alexander Jenkins. They can't take it away from him now, no matter what they do. I had to have that survey so I could tell the land office what I was buying and get the transaction established in the records."

"You redheaded devil!" Cal exclaimed admiringly. He stared at the papers unbelievingly, then started to return them to Johnny.

"Keep 'em," Johnny said. "Get 'em out to Alex just as fast as your horse will carry you. I've got business here in town. I'll come out to the house tonight —"

"Wait a minute," Cal said suddenly. "Did I hear you say you *bought* the property?"

"Sure, in Alex's name."

Cal looked troubled. "There's something wrong, Johnny, unless you're a millionaire in disguise. Why, the land alone must be worth around a hundred thousand dollars. You never owned that kind of money, did you?"

"Didn't say I used money," Johnny replied gleefully.

"Buttons, I suppose," sarcastically. "Now I know you've gone batty."

"Not buttons, either," Johnny explained. "Scrip."

"Scrip?" Cal frowned.

"Land certificates, bird-brain."

Cal shook his head. "I ain't sure I ever heard of 'em. Now that you mention it, though — Hell, Johnny, elucidate, will you?"

"Look, Cal," Johnny said. "I'll have to teach you a mite of history. After the Civil War the old state of Texas was pretty well broke financially. Texas didn't have money, but it did have land. So the state government in power at the time got the idea of issuing land certificates, calling for sections of open range to the extent of six hundred forty acres. I've heard a value was put on 'em of fifty cents an acre, but I'm not sure about that."

"Couldn't be. Too high a price."

"Maybe that's why the people didn't take to the idea of using such scrip in place of money. Nobody seemed to want the land certificates, and they became a drug on the market. The price dropped lower and lower, until they were selling at the rate of anywhere from two to five cents an acre — and not many buyers. But a few wise men bought them up whenever they could. My dad was one of those wise men. When he died he had a small tin chest just packed with scrip. I never thought much about that chest he'd willed to me. He had a heap better sense than me, I reckon. Then one day I was talking to Pat and I suddenly remembered that chest of scrip I'd left with a bank in San Antonio. I sent for it to be delivered to a bank in Austin. Remember? You mailed the letter for me. And so I used scrip that folks used to think was useless to buy Painted Post Valley — and I still got some scrip left too. What do you think of that?"

"Well, I'll be everlastingly damned!" Cal dropped weakly into a chair. His mind fumbled with mental mathematics. "Why — why — the Cross-J couldn't have cost much more than three thousand dollars if your dad bought in those land certificates at an average of three cents an acre."

"That just about hits it." Johnny nodded. "I'll tell you something else. Blaine and I checked on those farmers' leases in the land office. I always felt there was something funny about those leases. There is too. The land office never issued 'em! That means they're forgeries, probably signed by Malotte. I figure Cassidy or one of his pals stole the blank forms and filled 'em in themselves."

"I *will* be damned!" Cal shook his head in amazement.

"You probably will be if you don't fork your bronc pronto and get out to the Cross-J with this news. Give Pat my love."

Cal grinned widely. "You're sure riding high today, Johnny. Well, I'm on my way." He hurried out to the hitch rack, climbed into the saddle, and with a wild cowboy yell went tearing out of Painted Post, his exultant whoops startling people on the street. Hearing the yelling, Ben Cassidy came running from the Maverick Saloon just in time to see Johnny Auburn walking swiftly in the direction of the sheriff's office. A troubled expression crossed Cassidy's face as he turned back into the building.

Obie Grant was seated at his desk inside the office when Johnny arrived. He greeted Johnny enthusiastically, then said, "Did you see Cal? He just went past here whooping like a Comanche on the warpath. He must be drunk."

"He ain't" — Johnny laughed — "though he's got a good excuse for celebrating. So have I and you — and every other man who's stood out against Ben Cassidy and his gang."

"What is all this?" Obie asked. "I heard you'd gone to Austin — Urban told me you and Blaine were in there —"

"It adds up to one thing," Johnny broke in. "We've saved the Cross-J for Alex. . . ." From that point he took up the story and repeated what he had told Cal Henry, while Obie's eyes bugged farther and farther from his head.

"I'll be damned!" he exclaimed when Johnny had finished.

"That's what Cal said too. He looked like he was going to faint for a minute. Bear up and I'll tell you some more news."

"I hope it's good."

"It is. You're going to arrest Ben Cassidy for the murder of Sheriff Zach Robertson."

"That is good news," Obie snapped. "Give me details — and proof."

"Here's your proof. You know that day when I found Robertson's body he had been shot twice with a forty-five. I never told you before, Obie, but when I was looking for sign that day I found two forty-five shells near by, where the murderer had plugged them out of his gun. They were N.E.P. shells."

"That's good enough proof for me," Obie said angrily. "I know that Cassidy had some N.E.P.'s. It was N.E.P.'s he threw away that day —"

"I've done some investigating around town, Cassidy is the only man that ever used N.E.P.'s around here. The noose tightens around his neck a little more every minute."

"I'll go down now and make the arrest. He'll be in the Maverick. He's been running the place the last few days. Malotte's disappeared. I don't know where —"

"Wait, Obie, don't make that arrest until I tell you. Here's what I want you to do. You go down and see Cassidy. Tell him that you want him to bring all those farmers of his in town, that you got an announcement to make to them. If Cassidy wants to know what the announcement is don't tell him anything. Just say the announcement is coming through me and that it has to do with the land leases. I figure that will arouse his curiosity and that he'll do as you ask."

"But what's the idea?" Obie wanted to know.

"I don't want to have to waste time rounding up all those phony farmers. We'll get 'em in a bunch and tell 'em Cassidy's game is up and that they'd better leave town pronto or stay and be arrested as vagrants. Then you can arrest Cassidy. That'll show 'em they're finished. I figure to have you arrest Malotte too. Malotte will talk, I think, once he sees Cassidy is licked. We'll get all the evidence we need."

"The plan sounds all right." Obie nodded agreement. "I'll go now and tell Cassidy to get his farmers rounded up for a meeting."

He slapped on his Stetson and hurried from the office. Within ten minutes he was back.

Johnny asked, "What did he say?"

"Wanted to know where you had been. Tried to pump me, but I pretended not to know anything. Told him to get his gang in, that you had an announcement to make, through me, regarding the leases. That sure aroused his curiosity. He really started pumping then, but he didn't get a word out of me. He's plumb worried too; I could see that. But damn his killing hide" — Obie's eyes flashed dangerously — "it was all I could do to stop from arresting him right then."

"I'm glad you didn't. But what about the meeting? Will he get those riders in?"

"About two thirds of 'em are in town right now. Cassidy promised to send riders with word to the others. He's to let me know when they're all on hand."

"Good. When the time comes I'll prime you on what to say. Then we'll put the finish on Mister Ben Cassidy."

"And I hope he refuses to come quiet," Obie added grimly. "I'm sure honing to let daylight through his carcass!"

XXVII. Cassidy's Last Try!

Cold-Deck Malotte's face was tense with anxiety as he pushed his pony at a punishing gait toward Painted Post. The game was up now, he knew. By shadowing Johnny and Blaine around Austin and through discreet inquiries at the land office Malotte had learned exactly what had happened.

"Dammit!" he muttered as sage and brush and trees flowed past at a swift gait. "If only I hadn't missed that train that Auburn caught. Maybe I'd have had a good chance of pushing him off the end of a car or something. As it is, he's been in Painted Post four-five hours now. God only knows what's happened!" He struck the head of his pony savagely with his clenched fist. "Get on, you blasted crowbait. Can't you do anything but crawl?"

Malotte had several uncertain minutes while he considered turning the pony in the other direction and fleeing the Painted Post country as fast as possible. Some sense of loyalty to Cassidy kept him going, though, as well as thought of the money he'd put into the nefarious land-grab plan. In addition, there was his property, the Maverick Saloon. He just couldn't bring himself to abandon everything, without at least letting Cassidy know what was happening.

"Ben will get us out of this," he told himself hoarsely while the miles rapidly receded behind the flashing hoofs of the galloping pony. "Ben will think of something. He's smart. He's got us out of just as tough jams before. Dammit. He's got to get us out of this. I can't lose my money and the Maverick. Maybe we can round up our men and raid the Cross-J sometime when Auburn is there. Goddamn that redheaded Ranger! He's spoiled the whole business. If ever I get a chance to throw down on him . . . We could have handled the rest of the crowd. Geez, horse, show some speed, or I'll quirt your everlasting hide off your bones!"

Again he commenced beating the horse. The pony responded nobly, but by this time it had just about reached its limit.

Wild hopes, ideas surged through Malotte's hate-warped mind as he pushed the horse harder and harder. "Ben will sure be sunk when he hears we've lost the Cross-J. But we can lick Auburn yet if we work fast. We can shoot him in the back some night when he's going down the street. Next we'll raid the Cross-J — wipe out Jenkins and his daughter and the whole gang. We can fix it to look like some Indians been raiding. If we can

278

only get hold of that land deed — I can write out a bill of sale and forge Jenkins' name just as easy as I forged those leases. A quitclaim deed! That's what we need. I can write the name of Jenkins on a quitclaim just as easy as I wrote the moniker of that feller in the land office on the leases. Get along, horse! Run your damn hoofs off!"

With such thoughts, hopes, contradictions, and wild ideas flashing through his brain Cold-Deck finally came within sight of Painted Post. As he came tearing down Chisholm Street he saw a large number of overalled figures gathered in front of the Maverick Saloon. "Them's our men," Malotte muttered. "Cripes a'mighty! What's doing? Maybe Ben has already gathered them for a raid."

He stopped the pony at the edge of the crowd. Nobody had noticed him arriving. Malotte dropped from the pony to leave the exhausted animal swaying and straddle-legged. As he started for the porch at a dead run he noticed Johnny Auburn standing in the middle of the road, back of the crowd of assembled farmers.

Malotte started to push through the thick knot of men, trying to reach Ben Cassidy, whom he saw standing on the porch. Standing slightly in advance of Cassidy was Sheriff Obie Grant. Grant looked as if he was about to make a speech, or something.

Malotte fought his way through the crowd and reached one end of the porch. In two quick steps he was beside Cassidy and had pulled him to one side to whisper in his ear. Cassidy's face reddened at the words, then went white. Lines of baffled rage appeared in his features. He took one step toward Grant but suddenly stopped.

Obie had already started to speak as he stood gazing at the faces lifted toward him. "You fellers," Obie commenced slowly, "are probably wondering what I've called you here to say. Well, it's going to be short and sweet — short to you and sweet to me and every other law-abiding man in Painted Post. You all knew Jabez Vincent, I reckon. He was murdered by skunks. If there's any more of you fellers who expected to get land the way he did, what I'm going to say doesn't apply to you. But the rest had better gather their belongings and get clear of this county. Otherwise I'm arresting every man jack who stays."

An angry muttering ran through the crowd of so-called farmers.

Obie continued, hard-voiced, "I mean that! Ben Cassidy's game is finished here. Those leases for land were forged — not worth the paper they're written on. We know that now for certain."

"That's a damned lie!" Cassidy shouted. "By God! I'll shut your mouth, Grant!"

Drawing his gun, Cassidy triggered one savage shot into Obie's back, then turned and ran into the saloon, followed by Cold-Deck Malotte.

Malotte accused angrily, "You fool, Ben! What did you do that for? Now we are in for it."

Cassidy was white and trembling. "I lost my temper," he excused himself. "I know it was a fool move, Cold-Deck, but it just made me so damned mad — what you said and then hearing that blasted Grant —"

"All right, what you going to do now?" Cold-Deck said bitterly.

"They'll never take me alive!" Cassidy swore.

"How about me?" Malotte demanded.

"You can quit me if you like," Cassidy snapped. "Go on out and surrender. They'll let you off with a life sentence, maybe."

"Hell! I'm sticking, Ben!" Malotte said impulsively. He leaped over the bar, grabbed a shotgun, and hurried toward his back room. "Come on, we'll make a stand of it here."

Cassidy rushed after him. They slammed the door and bolted it.

Outside there was considerable confusion. An enraged muttering went up from several of the town's citizens who had gathered to hear what Obie was going to say. The crowd of farmers commenced to look uneasy. Several of them started to break away.

It had required several moments for Johnny to force his way through the crowd and reach the porch. He took one look at the silent form stretched on the porch floor, then stooped down and jerked the badge off Obie's shirt. Pinning the badge to his own vest, he raised his voice: "Somebody go round to the back and cut off Cassidy's escape. I'm going in after the back-shooting bustard!"

"Don't be a fool, Auburn," a townsman shouted. "Malotte is with him. It'll be two against one. Probably they'll hole up in Malotte's back room. You'll never take them alive!"

Johnny called back coldly as he started toward the saloon entrance: "Did I say I wanted them alive?"

He darted in between the swinging doors.

Inside the saloon was empty of men. Louie, the bartender, was probably outside someplace, making his getaway while the chance was right. Johnny's eyes flashed to the closed door at the back of the barroom. "It sure looks," he told himself, "as if I'd have to bust down a door!" He raised his voice: "You hombres coming out, or have I got to come in after you?"

There was no reply, though Johnny could hear low voices within the room.

He spoke again, his voice cuttingly contemptuous: "I knew you were yellow — but not this yellow. Come on, rats, take a chance! There's nobody else in here. It's my guns against yours. What do you say?"

Again no reply for a minute, then Malotte's voice: "We're waiting for you to come, lawman!"

Johnny hesitated, then slowly approached the door from one side. He tried the knob, found the door bolted from within. Two guns roared inside the room; twin slugs of lead ripped through the door panel. Fortunately Johnny wasn't standing directly before the door.

"You hombres had better do better than that." He laughed grimly. He strode up to the door, gave it a heavy blow with his booted foot, then leaped quickly to one side again.

Within the room a shotgun roared twice, the explosions almost blending. Buckshot sieved the flimsy door at numerous points. Like a flash Johnny opened fire with his forty-fives, the heavy leaden slugs cutting a savage pattern through the door. Malotte gave vent to a high-pitched scream, as his body struck the floor. Johnny again backed away, swiftly reloading his guns as he moved.

The street outside was filled with excited yelling. From the staccato drumming of horses' hoofs Johnny judged that a body of riders had arrived. He heard several shots out on Chisholm Street but had no time now to give them his attention. Probably some trouble with Cassidy's gang of fake farmers.

Johnny raised his voice. "It sounded like I got Malotte, Cassidy. It's you and me now. I got my coyote trapped at last."

Cassidy's reply came, savage, hateful: "Yeah, you got Cold-Deck, you redheaded devil! But you won't get me the same way. Stand back from that door. I'm coming out!"

Johnny gave a wild yell. "Got some nerve left, eh, Cassidy? Don't want to die like a rat in a trap. Come on, you murdering sidewinder. I won't shoot until you've seen me. Come with your guns a-smoking!"

He backed away from the door. The bolt clicked. Slowly the door swung open at first, then with a curse of rage Cassidy kicked it wide.

The six-shooters in his fists were spurting flame and hot lead almost before he sighted his target. Johnny swung himself to one side and felt the breeze of a bullet fan his left cheek. A second slug ripped through the neckerchief at his throat, slightly grazing the skin.

And then quite suddenly Johnny found himself on the floor in a sitting position. Through the haze of powder smoke he saw Cassidy rushing toward him, guns raised for another try. The guns swung down. Johnny felt red-hot irons strike through one shoulder and along his ribs. One of his arms felt lifeless now, but he raised the gun in his other hand and thumbed two swift shots.

He saw Cassidy sway back, catch his balance momentarily, then abruptly the man fell heavily to the floor.

They were both down now, Johnny in a sitting position, with both legs stretched out before him, and Cassidy struggling up to his knees.

Johnny felt himself growing weaker, but he managed a taunting laugh as he fought to raise his gun for another shot. Cassidy's six-shooter was coming up slowly too.

"It's your last try, Cassidy." Johnny grinned crazily. "You're my meat now."

"Damn you," Cassidy grated. "I'm taking you with me —"

The two shots crashed out at almost the same instant. Vaguely Johnny saw Cassidy crumple to one side as something struck him a heavy blow on the head. Shouts at the saloon entrance and a sudden rush of feet reached Johnny but dimly as he felt himself falling, falling; then everything went black in a deep sea of oblivion. . . .

XXVIII. Conclusion.

It was many days before Johnny opened his eyes again. When he did he found himself in a strange room — a strangely feminine room, in fact. He tried to move in the bed in which he found himself and experienced varied twinges of pain. He manipulated one arm and discovered bandages swathed about different portions of his anatomy. "This," he muttered drowsily, "is one hell of a fix. What happened? Where am I?"

There was a movement at the bedside. His mind cleared a trifle, and he saw Pat Jenkins bending over him. She said, "Oh, Johnny," in a hushed voice.

"Hello, lady," he greeted, and was shocked at the weakness of the tones.

"Hush," Pat said. "You've got to be quiet. Your fever's down at last. Now you must sleep and get back your strength again."

"Won't sleep," he mumbled stubbornly. "Want to know what happened."

"You'll sleep," she said severely. "Doctor's orders."

"Won't," he repeated. "Not until you've kissed me."

"That" — Pat smiled — "is one of the easiest things I can imagine doing."

He slipped off to sleep again, even while her lips were warm on his.

Several days slipped by, however, before Johnny was strong enough to talk to any extent. Gradually he learned that he had been brought out to the Cross-J and put to bed in Pat's room, because it was the coolest in the house. Dr. Kilburn came each day and finally allowed Johnny to sit up in bed and have visitors. They seemed to pour into the room as Pat helped Johnny to prop himself up on pillows.

Alex Jenkins came with his booming tones somewhat lowered, for probably the first time in his life, and Cal Henry and Yank Ferguson — in fact, the whole crew, led by Brazos Burnett — came trooping in to stand about his bed and voice congratulations on his recovery.

Johnny looked from face to face, then asked, "How about Obie Grant?"

Pat replied, "Obie will live, though he had a mighty narrow escape. He's staying at Doc Kilburn's; they don't dare move him. Shucks, cowboy, the plugging you got is nothing to what Obie received, though you won the edge on quantity. We weren't sure you'd live —"

"Cassidy?" Johnny broke in.

"Cassidy is dead," Cal Henry replied, "for

which glad tidings you're probably as thankful as we are. Likewise, you should be considerably cheered by the voicing of such information, and considering the proposition that —"

Johnny interrupted dryly, "The fact that he's dead suits me, Cal. You don't need to go into details."

"Look here," Alex Jenkins said seriously, "you don't know how I feel, and I'm not going to tell you right now — it would take too long — but you saved the Cross-J —" He paused, his eyes a trifle moist, then: "Hell's bells, boy! It's your place now. I can't accept it. You shouldn't have put that deed in my name."

"Alex" — Johnny smiled — "if I hadn't wanted it that way I wouldn't have done it."

"But you're throwing away a fortune. Do you realize what this land cost — this land you're *giving* me."

"Gosh, Alex," Johnny pleaded, "let's forget it."

"I won't forget it!" Alex thundered. "There's going to be a new deed made out. You'll take a half interest or I'll take nothing! Do you hear?"

Johnny grinned. "You've got to throw in Pat to boot."

"Boot her all over the place, if you like!" Alex boomed. "I've been intending to boot her or shoot her for some time. Me, I'm done with Pat. Any time a redheaded jasper comes along and makes her listen to him, 'stead of me, I know I'm licked. I'll be glad to get rid of the hussy, so long as you leave her here."

"Dad" — Pat laughed — "I won't be bargained for."

Johnny chuckled. "Shut up, friend. This is between Alex and me. You haven't a thing to say, unless you have more news to pass out. Say, how about Malotte?"

"Malotte," said Brazos Burnett, "will live to serve a long sentence. Your shot just knocked him out for a spell. Johnny, that skunk sure talked when we put pressure on him. You see, it was Malotte's idea, in the first place, to steal the Cross-J. He financed the proposition after he learned from county records that the Cross-J valley was still considered open range. He got in touch with his old pal Cassidy, and they hired a gang of thugs to pose as farmers. Someplace, somehow, they stole those lease forms, and Malotte, who is quite handy with a pen, forged those leases."

"Figuring, I suppose," Alex Jenkins growled, "that I'd just move out without a fight and leave them the Cross-J. Once they had the place, they planned to set up a real rustling business here and steal cows not only from neighboring ranchers, but from all the trail herds that came through here on their way to Dodge City. But you stopped the scuts,

Johnny! That scrip idea of yours was a jim-dandy! Lord, I haven't seen one of those old land certificates for years now. I guess the wise men, like your father, bought 'em up in the old days, when nobody would have anything to do with 'em. I remember I had one of those certificates once. Traded a cow for it, carried it around several months, then traded it to another feller for a bowie knife I liked. I've seen those certificates used in poker games, too, when there wasn't any money floating around —"

"Something else Malotte told us," Cal Henry broke in. "It was Ben Cassidy who shot Sheriff Robertson all right. Dry-gulched Robertson on the trail, then laid Robertson's shotgun with the two exploded shells in it beside the body. When you came along Mitch Bailey was supposed to blow hell — I mean the daylights — out of you with his shotgun, Johnny. The idea being, of course, when your body and Robertson's were found, folks would think you and the sheriff had quarreled and killed each other. It was well known that Robertson didn't want a Ranger coming in here."

"It was Tascosa Jake who killed Jabez Vincent that night," Yank Ferguson put in.

"Speaking of Vincent," Pat said, "there was a letter came from his wife up in Arkansas. I hated like sin to do it, but I took on the job of breaking the news to the poor kid. Dad fixed things up so the sale of Malotte's saloon will give her some money to live on. The way Dad put it to Malotte, Malotte was more than glad to fall in with the idea, in hope of getting a lighter sentence when he comes up for trial."

"That's fine." Johnny nodded. "What happened to that gang of sidewinders that called themselves farmers?"

Cal Henry answered, "We took care of them the same day you killed Cassidy. You see, when I got to the Cross-J and gave Alex the deed to his land and told him and Pat how you'd worked it, Alex decided we'd all come to town and give you a guard of honor back to the ranch."

"No more than you deserved!" Alex thundered. "Pat insisted on coming too. Well, we got to Painted Post just about the time you were crossing guns with Cassidy and Malotte. When we learned what happened to Obie Grant we quick rounded up those fake farmers and ordered 'em to get out! There were a few scrappy ones among 'em, but we burnt some powder under their noses and took the fight out of 'em. Cal and me made a rush inside the Maverick, only to find both you and Cassidy stretched on the floor. Malotte was unconscious in his back room, but we brought him to in a little spell and —"

"Anyway," Pat broke in, "things are pretty well settled up, Johnny, due to you." She turned to the others. "Time to leave, fellers. Johnny has to catch some more sleep. He must have rest and quiet."

"Can't be done with you around," Alex chuckled. "He looks to me like he gets a rise in temperature every time you come nigh him."

"Dad!" Pat blushed. "You get out of here right now. All of you get! Scat!"

They "scatted."

Pat closed the door behind them and returned to sit on the bed beside Johnny. "I forgot to tell you before," she said. "There was a letter came for you from your Captain Travis of the Rangers. I figured it might be important, so took the liberty of opening it. Captain Travis wants to know if you can't be persuaded to return to the Rangers and — in his own words — 'what the hell happened up here?' "

"Write to him for me," Johnny said softly. "Tell him I have a range of my own and a new captain named Pat. Tell him I may even have my own company of Texas Rangers before many years —"

"Johnny!" Pat's cheeks crimsoned and she smothered further words with her warm lips.

There was silence for a few moments; then Johnny chuckled. "But, Pat, it's all for the glorious state of Texas. Can you think of a better way to keep down crime?"

Pat admitted she couldn't. She admitted

other things, too, but they were for Johnny's ears alone, things that concerned only the two of them and had nothing to do with Rangers — rebel or otherwise.

The employees of Thorndike Press hope you have enjoyed this Large Print book. All our Thorndike and Wheeler Large Print titles are designed for easy reading, and all our books are made to last. Other Thorndike Press Large Print books are available at your library, through selected bookstores, or directly from us.

For information about titles, please call:

(800) 223-1244

or visit our Web site at:

www.gale.com/thorndike
www.gale.com/wheeler

To share your comments, please write:

Publisher
Thorndike Press
295 Kennedy Memorial Drive
Waterville, ME   04901